OFF SUNSET

I Can Hear 'em Laughing

ADAMSON GREGORY

CONTENTS

SUNDAY NIGHT

11:23 P.M.

A chilling midnight breeze overtook the necks of those in line outside The Comedy Store. West Hollywood was lively and the line-up was strong as ever. The bright bulbs surrounding the building's rooftop seemed to flicker with every burst of wind across the night sky.

"Ey man. You know who's in the Belly Room right now?" asked a patron from the back of the line.

"Nah, sorry," replied Eddie. Eddie Mason had been working the front door for almost three years and just about every time he felt hopeless or that he wasn't making any progress in his career, something would happen and pull Eddie right back into comedy's vice-like clutches. Whether it was a better shift or a fancy face at the door, something unresolved called to him like a siren in the night. Since birth he was a funny kid and unsurprisingly he found himself trying to be a class clown professionally. Although that may not sound like a courageous undertaking——he remained lionhearted. Eddie found inspiration in everyday people and his act had been sculpted over time in that image. Those around him had very high hopes. Kurt the security guy stepped past him to light up a cigarette at the front door.

"Hey Kurt, who's up right now in the Belly Room?" asked Eddie. Kurt finished his long drag on the cigarette.

"Patrice! He's goin' back to New York tomorrow with a few other guys I guess so he wanted to get a spot in. Maron's in the Main right now and he's killing it. Then Giraldo's starting a fire in the Original....yo, you see Mitch last night?" he replied before finishing with a question.

"Mitch fucking Hedberg was here last night? When?" shot back Eddie, knowing every head that walked into the building over the last 72 hours.

"No man. On Letterman. That dude is fucking hilarious," said Kurt. Eddie echoed that same sentiment in his head just as another patron stepped forward and presented their ID.

"Two drink minimum guys remember. Have a good time," he said before waving them into the solid red wall of entry-lights. With each step they engulfed in the vibrant neon rays of red fighting the moon's blue across every fold of cloth and solid surface within reach like a Robert Yarber painting come to life.

"Hey I know you! Yeah, I saw you here two nights ago

at like one in the morning," shouted the next girl in line. Eddie chuckled in reflection of such a terrible time-slot but thankfully, tonight was a little different, or so he thought.

"Yeah that sounds like me. What'd you think? Did'ya have a good time?" he asked, reaching out with the stamp.

"We had a great time! And you had one about your kid-bike. That was so funny, oh my god," she replied.

He thanked them even though the patron seemed to be dissembling the truth. To Eddie, people always kiss ass at the door unless they're being actively told no. For whatever it's worth, that was at least a common trend, most people just acted happier and or more successful than they actually were. On the other hand, when you see that many people on a nightly basis like Eddie did, your radar for a fake smile becomes crystal clear and penetrating. The rest of the night seemed all the same. Two or three folks thrown out for poor behavior by the big Kurt but other than that it was a dull shift for a stargazer surrounded by stars. AM struck abruptly. Eddie was relieved from his post at the door with the tap of his shoulder. Inside he soaked in the crimson lights before leaning up against the merch-booth table.

"Eddie! How's it hangin' bud?" shouted Bruce Latto, Eddie's coworker, friend and another up-and-coming comic. "Low and to the left?" he finished.

"Somethin' like that," returned Eddie before continuing. "I'm up in a bit, just enough time to get a lil buzz on so I'm gonna head to the bar but you tryna...?" he said pinching his thumb and forefinger together against his lips. Eddie hadn't seen a smile like that all night. Bruce pulled a sign out of his ass that said "Gon' Shittin'" and placed it on the merch-booth table.

The dark corridors of the Comedy Store could be walked through while blindfolded for both these two yet every step they took and every turn they made, a new wonder would shine out. Peeking through doors as they passed, that feeling of show business wafted the air around them like thick ash after a forest fire. First was the Main Room, a sophisticatedly dressed stage with the classic and classy light pageantry only fitting for the biggest and most famous of all three platforms within the Comedy Store.

Next there was the Original Room, a smaller yet stylishly arranged space with tables and chairs scattered around and lit by neon signs on every wall.

Finally up a confined and dark set of stairs there's the Belly Room, a very personal space that could also be called the Elbow Room with it's low light and chairs lined shoulder to shoulder in front of only the mic stand and a humble curtain. With less of a stage and more of a placemat, it offered an intimate opportunity to speak freely on a level that can only be described as eye-to-eye.

Eddie and Bruce burst through the back door to smoke a joint in the parking lot. The sound from the Original Room could be heard from out on the pavement and before they sparked up Bruce ushered their ears in, to eavesdrop.

"Yeah so I'm gay... So if you girls wanna scooch back a little bit I totally understand. Actually, you know what? You all can leave, all the women in the audience can just leave cuz honestly there's nothing here for you," said the voice followed by a bevy of laughter. Bruce smiled with a peculiar look in his eyes. "Kills every time. I don't get it," he said, commenting on the varied tastes within what people find funny, before being cut off by the lighter's flick. Eddie took a liberal inhale as if he was in a hurry and held in the smoke while passing to Bruce. When Bruce was done it was meticulously snatched from his clutches by a handful of long, french-tipped fingernails. Penny Peterson, a talented stand-up peer of theirs.

"You fuckers holding out on me. I gots'ta get mine, yo," she said facetiously before suddenly slapping Eddie in the chest. One of her rings caught a bone near his sternum and pounded out like a drum. "Heard you got a couple minutes tonight! Congrats. Congrats," she said.

"Yeah, I'll be up in a few," he said grabbing the joint and taking another mondo toke, then another. "Somebody had a kid-thing I guess so I was able to take their 12:30 slot," said Eddie.

"You deserve it man. If I was in charge you'd be billed at the tippy-tippy top! You'd already have a signature on the wall bro front and center by the door," joked Bruce reaching back for the joint. The signature he was referring to was a symbol of success in the Los Angeles comedy scene where after an aspiring comedian works long and hard enough at the Comedy Store as a doorman etc then they would eventually get picked up as what is called a Paid Regular. A main player lifted from the bench and placed as part of the main roster at which point said person's name is painted on the side of the black building's exterior next to the greats that came before them. The emotion caused by seeing your own name on the side of the Comedy Store was enough to fill Pyramid Lake with tears of joy and excitement and Eddie wished that future to be true. He exhaled through his nostrils and then walked back inside and picked up a drink from the bar to hype himself up before heading to the green room.

11:59 P.M.

Outside, Penny and Bruce were still smoking and talking. They discussed feelings on the current climate in stand up, especially in LA and the troubles of finding time and space on stage...

"That dude's fuckin funny man," Penny said, taking a long drag while admiring his perseverance.

"Seriously. Eddie's great. He'll find it, they all just need to see it," professed Bruce.

"He finish the punch for that joke yet?" she asked. "Not yet," he returned with a laugh. Penny grabbed what was left of the joint and then asked: "How's tonight? Anybody poppin' off?"

"Crowd's pretty good. Patrice swung by earlier so you know he threw down but yeah. Joey Diaz was workin' on some stuff, he actually had a few extra minutes tonight which was cool. Fuckin' Karl, he's always up to somethin'. And then Genie came out swinging as always," answered Bruce before almost being cut off by Penny.

"Does she *ever* miss?!" she exclaimed.

"Never," returned Bruce.

"And you can tell Karl to eat my ass. He still here?" she asked, walking towards the door.

"You'll see'em," shouted Bruce, looking down at his beeper.

12:15 A.M.

Eddie stepped over a piece of trash on the pavement and his pothead mind started to dawdle as his feet hit cruise-control.

One of the Comedy Store's great burdens wasn't of idiosyncratic societal-issues or distinctively tied to the negativity towards the competitive nature between peers within a work place, but of the workplace itself. The Comedy Store is a machine, one that while well-oiled will run a mile a minute and leave anyone behind who was not already on board.

Yet a machine requires care, maintenance, and an almost endearing relationship to continue on running smoothly. When stepping through those hallowed doors, what may look like a court's jester spewing nonsensical poetry into a metal rod is actually but a cog dedicating itself to said machine, greasing the gears of the locomotive with giggles and sections for thought, before leaving every whimsy-induced passenger with a lasting memory or message or both if they're lucky. It may not sound like much of a burden but when the lights go down and the streets are filled with silence, optimism becomes less of a social norm and more of an uphill battle not worth fighting. Most people don't or simply won't challenge themselves to a laugh nor do they see the benefit in doing so. People wander aimlessly for a majority of their lives, searching for happiness until stumbling upon the virtuous craft of comedy, either as a passenger or as one of the cogs. That is why it is the Store's duty and unspoken obligation along with many other Cellars and Factories like it, to abstain from that silence. To resist the chivalrous deference towards pessimism and ride a wave of challenging insecurity towards a far from commissioned guffaw. Will it require hard work and dedication? Absolutely. Will it be easy in any sense of the word? Absolutely not. But what is left will be a fine-tuned mechanism ready for all and afraid of none, that much is certain.

Inside, Eddie widened his eyes hoping to corral his pupils back into proper size and position. He smiled at a busser and started walking towards the tables in the rear of the room. With each strafe of his pant leg across the other as he walked, Eddie hoped and prayed that he was the only one hearing it.

"Hey kid! Finally getting some minutes, how about that?" shouted Gilbert Gottfried. Behind and around him sat: Genie Santiago, Karl Phan and Pauly Shore, son of the owner Mitzi. All established comedians with over a decade under their respective belts. They were shooting the shit and Pauly was telling Eddie to breathe *buuuuddy*.

On the main stage was Leland Poe. An opener for the hot shots mentioned previously. Leland had a unique act as it was primarily crowd work with little to no written material. The more seasoned stand-ups weren't all fans of his work but respected the laughs he got regardless; although, a majority of his success was always attributed to his looks. They chopped it up before Eddie peaced out to head upstairs. He sat down next to Greg Giraldo.

"Sup dude! Mitzi got with you right?" asked Greg, dangling a glass of ice between his thumb and pinky.

"Nah, whatsup?" replied Eddie with only half of his attention.

"Aubrey's here. So he's going first and you've got five now. Sorry brotha," Greg said and stood up to walk away. Eddie looked down into his drink, finally processing the news. Whoever was currently onstage had become blurred and silent. Their act was ongoing yet Eddie couldn't hear a thing. Suddenly he felt another tap on his shoulder and two bodies sat down next to him. It was Penny and Bruce.

"Fuck that guy, man. If that prick wanted time up there, he should've shown up like everybody else. Asshole," shouted Penny, referring to Clark.

Bruce shook his head and said "I mean, you're not wrong." Then there was a tap on *his* shoulder. Karl leaned into Bruce's ear and Bruce shot up.

"He's here?" he expelled like a child on Christmas then followed Karl to the green room. "Screw you Karl! Don't worry about him. He had *ONE* special twelve years ago. SO the fuck what," said Penny.

Eddie finished his drink and then walked to the back. Filling the room was an air of cigarette smoke and the stars were circling like vultures above a still-beating heart. There sat Aubrey Clark, the clean comic global extraordinaire. He had just got back from a big tour, a part in a major movie and returned like a graduate the year after. His smile said it all. Karl sat down next to him with another verbal reminder to the room of how they came up together. After starting out in Georgia they moved to New York and then eventually tinseltown. On the other side was Colin Quinn, an old friend from college and star in his own right. They came up on stage together in New York so Colin came along with a few other East Coast comics to support his old pal.

"Eddie!" shouted Aubrey, "Thank you so much man I really appreciate it," his hand out-stretched to shake. Eddie obliged and thanked him as if he had a choice in the matter. He made his way over to the stage entrance and was met by Gilda Bean, an astoundingly talented comedian and actor in ribaldry.

"Don't hate me," she said, sinking Eddie's brow like the Titanic in cold water. "It's three now. I'm sorry dude, it wasn't my call I'm just the one tellin' you. But listen, you're gonna kill it. Go get'em!" she said enthusiastically then waved him out into the lights. As Eddie approached the stage he wiped the visual emotion off his face before the stage lights hit him before shoving himself forward, flailing about before turning back as if he was thrown onstage. He adjusted himself and patted his thighs before awkwardly grabbing the mic and said nervously,

"They uh. They make me come up here and vent about my sleep-paralysis demon." Eddie looked off-stage and flinched as if a missile was inbound then carried on with his set like a subjugated animal.

"I used to be a bartender, like my mom, but I don't think I have the quick-thinking skills necessary for the job. It's a lot of counting and giving change and I keep getting fired for spilling the margaritas every time I try to put salt on the rim...

The drinks are perfect as far as I can tell but as soon as I flipped'em over and dip it in the salt; the drink goes everywhere, I have to remake it, and it ruins the salt!" he said sending the front row into eye-rolls and covered laughter. Eddie continued:

"Do you know how much salt I've had taken out of my paycheck? Better yet, do you know how hard it is to explain *that* many salt purchases let alone deductions when I'm doing taxes at the end of the fiscal? I was glad they fired me man, let me fly off like a caterpillar in the night.

But look, you can get away with it a handful of times at say a Mexican restaurant because they got a bunch of salt in the back, but when you work in the bar at a cracker-barrel... and I don't even mean the restaurant I just mean a white establishment, they only have a finite amount of salt and that shit might as well be currency the way they hold on to it.

It's not in the food, it's not in the register! Is it in the safe?! Safeguarding salt. For what...?

So that I can fuck up more margaritas!

But mira, escuchan!

There's only so far a manager can let shit slide in non-slip shoes and only so much you can sweep under a rug. Think about it, anyone in here who's been a manager, how many rugs do you see in a bar?

Exactly! None!

So after there's too much to be swept-up or in my case mopped-up they tell me to piss off and go lick bricks. So I did what they told me and I was peeing outside a building trying to see if I could lick it too when I looked up and saw a sign that said free open mic and that's why I'm here! Thank you!"

As that was happening a voice raised backstage.

"Hey big boy!" shouted Leland as he walked into the green room.

"Kid! I heard you were schooling people tonight. Is that true?" asked Aubrey in return. "Of course," shouted Leland without hesitation. They shook hands like old friends. Leland then reminded everyone he hit a few shows along with Aubrey on the latest tour. A few faces continued sniffing Aubrey Clark's ass and the rest paid attention to Eddie on stage.

12:36 A.M.

"Ladies and lads, boys an goyles... Mr. Aubrey Clark!" Eddie lowered the mic and handed it to Aubrey as he walked off stage. He patted Eddie's shoulder and cleared his throat.

"Eddie Mason everybody! Give it up. Shoot! It's good to be back upstairs in the abortion clinic," blurted out Aubrey before continuing, already in a bit of a sweat from the Belly Room's sweltering stage lights. Eddie was surrounded backstage.

"Bro that was slick!" whispered Bruce.

"Haven't seen that one before. I was out at the bar excited and caught it *all* that was fuckin' great," shouted Penny. Genie Santiago agreed with high praise.

"Nice job dude," mumbled the soft voice of Jim Gaffigan, leaning forward from his seat with his fist out to bump and then soon it was closing time and sweeping needed to be done. The younger guys and girls usually stayed to help clean up and also show face amongst the remaining company of established comedians, stars and Mitzi. All patrons that weren't a paid regular or a celebrity of sorts were kicked out, and it was then a private party, so to speak. Down in the Main Room some cleaning still to be done but celebrities and the paid regulars were standing around staring at the stage with the last of their drinks.

"Hey Mitzi! Remember I told you about the Hollywood diaries? Eddie, come up here. Mitzi, let Eddie tell everybody a story before we go home," pleaded Genie into the mic. She was lucky the room was already on high but Mitzi agreed with quickness. When Mitzi really trusts someone it shows in times like these, when your work is worth trusting your word. Genie had that in spades and used it in times like these to not only give Eddie back his minutes but to let him show everyone what he's really about. Eddie took the stage and plainly asked which one. The room chuckled but Eddie didn't seem to know what to do with his hands and that was noticed too.

"Tell'em the one about Hollywood and your Dad ya dummy!" shouted Penny and Bruce, almost like proud parents twice removed.

"Coolio thanks. Bruce Latto everybody! The man with an eighty year old man's name yet he's fucking thirty-four. And speaking of having thirty four kids, Aubrey Clark! He's seemingly become the new dad on TV; I heard through a reliable seagull or two that he's even being talked about for the father fish in a new animated Disney picture so let's give it up for paps! Let's hope they don't animate you as a flounder fish——or an asshole," said Eddie into the mic and referring to a to-be-announced Pixar movie about two clown fish. In that moment the room seemed to brighten from all the fake teeth being flashed through tight lips stretched ear to ear.

Bruce stood up and claimed to be only thirty before sitting back down befuddled with embarrassment. Eddie noticed Bruce try to regress into the small crowd after heckling so he dug in.

"Okay hold on, Bruce if you're thirty then that makes Leland the same age as the baby from *Look Who's Talking*, and I don't think I'm mature enough to accept that," Eddie responded, to a welcoming of warm laughter of all ages as he crossed the cold, thin ice of movie references.

"But oh yeah, the Hollywood Diaries yet it's more of a mutha-fuckin' diorama," Eddie said while waving out his arm at the audience with a pseudo-enthusiastic presentation. "That one worked, tight," he whispered and glanced down at his palm non-discretely. Regardless of whether or not it got a laugh he would pretend to check his palm every time."Apologies for swearing in front of Ellen by the way but this is kinda just how I talk so....deal with it." Eddie pointed at Aubrey Clark laughing with his mouth full in the make-shift crowd. Those around him were pointing at him with cupped palms silencing their laughter.

"Fuck sorry, okay. So I am third-generation Hollywood once removed. Which basically means I was cheated. And I don't mean like having to see Bobby Lee naked over-and-over-again cheated but you know pretty fucking cheated. Let me explain... For reasons I cannot explain, my paternal grandfather's family moved to Hollywood from Minnesota just before he hit high-school, preferring the company of the cold blooded assholes in LA over the warm. He went to Hollywood High School and went on to form a band...

A decade prior, my paternal grandmother's family had just settled into a new home in the hills off Sunset, across the street from where the Playboy building would eventually erect. Pun intended...

In those days it was black-and-white but the middle class could earn a living without care in the studios, it was Hollywood in the 1930's. Nanna's dad ran the *Long's Drugs* on Sunset there, and when my Nanna was a little girl, she would play with Shirley Temple every time her and her mom would come in to the Pharmacy. They became fast friends until Shirley Temple's career took off.

Nanna grew up halfway up that windy hill and then passed through Hollywood High School all the same. She too found herself in the arts and although she never made it to even five feet tall she had the highest voice of all singers in the choir and could reach a C above C as they say."

All eyes were on Eddie Mason. Although instinctually funny, he wasn't knocking on doors for laughs. He had started to find himself as a comedian simply through telling stories and what was deemed the gift of gab in his formative years had become his greatest strength. He had them captivated, putty in his hand, and he was pretty sure he knew it.

"In a crazy exchange of events called life, Nanna found herself a husband in Paps and his band. They formed a Quartet and did well enough to have been on the original Peter Pan theme song, Oklahoma! and that one tiki shit at Disneyland with all the singing birds.

You know? Parrots, pecans, parakeets and geese? One of those is a nut, but they all stare into your soul and croon? You know the one..."

Suddenly Gilda, the elder, shouted out with enlightenment: "It's the Enchanted Tiki Room, shit-ass!" The room broke with laughter as did Eddie but he regained composer like a pro and continued with the additive engagement.

"Ya that was them! Soon they got noticed by another man and agreed to join his forming choir known as The Ray Conniff Singers. You ever see the little short lady, with black pompadour hair and the dude that looks like me? Yeah. That's them!

Well they went on and had two sons of their own so now we're in the 1950's. They're married, husband and wife with three rambunctious boys, all three grow up in the Lloyd Wright house on Ogden Drive just off Sunset down there. All three went to Hollywood High School and by the 1960's the eldest son was leading the choir at the Methodist church back up the street and sang alongside a young John Ritter. Him and his two younger brothers joined their parents to stand and sing in the choir on the Dean Martin show on a few occasions. As a family! Then the eldest joined the Navy and advanced to the rank of Captain. The middle brother followed suit long after and went on to become a Petty Officer First Class but not before his Senior year at Hollywood High where he was in the same graduating class as Jermaine Jackson of the Jackson 5. He would even wait at the stairs after school for a quick pickup from the parents. All the while, the youngest brother, my Dad, would brush past their youngest brother, a young Michael Jackson performing Karate chops through air to telepathically usher his own older brother to come to the car. Before graduation my Dad found himself sneaking over the fence and watching The Beatles perform at The Hollywood Bowl but when he was sixteen his Dad died and their Mom found a new-man, from her past. Her high school sweetheart turned conman extraordinaire, and after a few months for reasons unknown he lost the deed to two different Hollywood houses in a bad bet. Life finds a way doesn't it? Even when you don't want it to. Gramps gave me a handful of pennies in a Ralph's bag for Christmas one year, they forgot about my sister so Nanna stepped out of her own beaten old slippers and handed them over. Interesting people...

Fast forward a few years and my Dad's now working in the studios as a Special Effects guy and doing pretty well. He famously got along so well with Robin Williams they seemed like long-lost pals on the set of HOOK and at one point they convinced the make up department to dress them both up like Hasidic Jews transported from either Lancaster, Pennsylvania or right off 83rd Street & Amsterdam Ave in the upper west side of New York. So it's Robin Williams and my Dad walking around yapping in yiddish and throwing judgmental blessings towards everyone on set until lunch was over and it was back to work, oy vey.

He met my Mom and they had me and my sister

and then he ran off to get cigarettes as the saying goes so my poor mother had to move with her two kids to the only place in California she could still afford outside of Riverside and Bakersfield. So just before High School we wound up moving to bum fuck Fresno. Have you ever been to Fresno?

No.

Wanna know how I know?

I can smell it on your breath.

It comes from your pores like fucking cold-cuts on a hot summer day... in Fresno. It's like, you ever been in an elevator and someone farted? How awkward that is right? Trapped in a sarcophagus of ass. Now imagine it's not a fart and it's an actual fucking cow. And you have to just act like there's not a farm animal pushing its asshole up against you so it doesn't have to squeak up against the smudged elevator doors again. All I'm sayin is it doesn't take a Detective okay? It stinks mmkay?

So I moved back here after High School instead of joining the Navy and you know why? Revenge... for the teen years I missed in this whore-house of a city.

The useless celebrity connections and nonsensical networking.

I came back to baptize myself in mescaline and laughs on Sunset Boulevard like it's the Lake of Mina-fuckin-tonka and PRINCE doesn't even go here!

But you know being the kid of a guy in the movie business has its perks, outside of sweeping this very floor here my dad was never home and was always away for work so he taught me a vigorous work ethic. Always get it done...

I remember when I was probably 8 or 9 he was telling me as I held his cigarette how they used to be able to pull off giant set builds overnight like the ice-cube making machine in Back to the Future III. He'd say you start drinking whiskey and after the whiskey isn't keeping you up anymore then you do a line of coke so you stay up and build, drink a little more then a do another line, starting the process over again until the sun rises and the set is built. If you think that's bad, let me tell you something, they used to pay you in coke. Not only that, most of the producer parties just had mountains of cocaine centering their coffee tables as a party gift upon arrival. FOR FREE upon arrival!

I can't imagine being donated an illegal substance let alone something *of* substance AND being invited to a party? What a score.

Dude the last time I got something for free it was *advice* and it was terrible, I almost walked out into traffic!

Okay, they're calling me off guys. Thanks, I'm not getting paid for this by the way but I will accept sexual favors. Please see me after the show..." finished Eddie with a dry whit. The room had been loud along the way and he found his route out in the best way possible, at the top.

3:00 A.M.

The night was over and Aubrey unexpectedly left his group and approached Bruce and Eddie to chat. He laid on some thick spiel, somewhere in between a guys' night out and getting kicked out of the house, all to invite himself over. Once the last of the cleaning and closing was complete, they all hopped into Bruce's station wagon and made their way to his studio apartment in Burbank. The door couldn't have slammed shut and locked quicker only to discover that the power was out. The three men sat on the foldable couch with a candle and lit up a joint by the window. Eddie wasn't aware Aubrey smoked weed nor did he expect Mr. Clark to now be passing him the joint. America's new sweetheart. The guy's face was literally on the side of the bus stop outside the apartment. Eddie noticed a trail burning down one side of the joint paper and fixed it. They burnt it to nothing as the candle's flame threw shadows around the room. A cold came about, tales of flickering fury played across the bare walls and the three men relinquished their road stories.

"Was all that the truth? On stage.." asked Aubrey before being offered a drink by Bruce. He declined and reminded them both that he quit drinking long ago and only quietly kept smoking weed. *California sober* as he calls it. Bruce chastised himself for forgetting and then he and Eddie did a final shot of whiskey for the night before sitting back down and Aubrey re-asked his question. Eddie thought for a second, as if confused that Aubrey really gave a shit.

"Absolutely. If you've seen Back to the Future III, when they're in the barn and that part shoots out from the bottom of the DeLorean? That was him laying under the car, chucking it out on cue.

I left a bit out though, like my dad fingering the chick from *Gunsmoke* but hey that's showbiz right?" he joked with a wink that cracked the room. Aubrey leaned in and Eddie swayed over in his high. "That was some pretty good stuff though, if not a little long. I'd say add some more pops in the beginning so they don't just think you're giving a speech. What have you been doing? Fifteen?" asked Aubrey. Eddie looked out the window with squinted eyes. Whatever had pseudo-stolen his attention had vanished just as quickly. He itched his ear and said "When I'm not getting bumped? Five."

"What?" shouted Aubrey after a repeat back.

"I mean I'll do ten or thirteen fairly often too but on bigger nights it's usually just three or five or I'm just the MC, honestly," admitted Eddie and just like that, Bruce inserted himself.

"Fuck right off! You are the preferred MC and you know it. You smash, you just have bad timing—wait, not on stage I just mean in life—fuck! I mean you do well just not when people are there watching. You know what I'm trying to say!" Bruce stuttered into the sea of deadly stares coming his way.

"Yeah that I suck!" added Eddie with a glance over at Aubrey trying to catch his breath.

"No! Brother c'mon. You know I think you're the

funniest fucking guy I know. He helps literally every single stand up at the Store punch up shit when they have gone through everything they have. We all come to him," ranted Bruce looking over at Aubrey like the room's unbiased mediary. He directed his gaze back towards Eddie and then his inebriation started to show.

"You just always get bad slots my man. I don't make the slots I just take'em and the ones that *you* get given are all when nobody's around, even a killer spot sometimes and fuckin' Mitzi will go take a shit right before Eddie gets announced. I'm sure it's not planned but holy shit does it happen..." Bruce paused and Eddie picked it up for him:

"A lot."

"I mean Mitzi might just have a routine bowel schedule. Not even a good joke can stop that," said Aubrey with a casual grin. Bruce and Eddie laughed as Aubrey was now motioning for another joint even though he would only take a few puffs and leave the rest for them. They got excited and Bruce retrieved it.

"How long's he been in the studios? Your father," asked Aubrey out of nowhere.

"Since, uhm, since the mid-seventies. His step-brother was an FX man and was working on JAWS at the time and his shop was gearing up for The Incredible Hulk series, I think? Anyways he got my dad a gig and it was history from there," responded Eddie, neglecting to affirm the shock within himself that Aubrey fucking Clark was asking about his dad because of a bit at the Store.

"He work on anything I'd know?" asked Aubrey,

almost admitting interest out of the blue. "Of course, yeah. He did the shower-torture scene and the final scene in Scarface, Back to the Future 2 and 3 as Effects Coordinator but maybe just as a lead technician, he did Hook with Robin Williams and Dustin Hoffman, tons of stories on that, Indian in the Cupboard, Basic Instinct, shit he would say he did Knight Rider for so long that him and David Hasselhoff became pretty good friends. He'd tell me stories about walking down the street in Culver City or wherever and he'd see a red convertible Corvette drive by and would immediately know who it was. It would whip a U-turn and Hasselhoff would skid sideways on the street to park at the curb in front of him and then just yell 'HEY GREG!'"

"You serious? I did Knight Rider a few times! I had a three episode arc in the final season, what must've been '85? What a coincidence. Seriously that's pretty insane. The world's smaller than ya think," said Aubrey. Eddie was feeling possibly more comfortable than he needed to be and blurted out a thought:

"I'd ask if you remember a short, tan dude with tattoos on his forearms and a cigarette in his mouth but that pretty much describes any one of the crew back then. Only difference was Marlboro or Winston."Aubrey chuckled to himself and said, "You're telling me. I remember sitting in a tiny, tiny room with a paper wall separating us from the casting director and actual audition and the whole room was just thick with smoke. You couldn't see your hand in front of your face even if you smacked your forehead. All those cats looking to make it big but so darn nervous that they practically had a non-stop rotation of nicotine in hand at all times, indoors and out. What's even crazier is a few of those cats are big lions in the industry now, you know. It's all cyclical. I remember I was doing a pilot in the early 90's—ah, maybe it was late 80's. Either way, I'm sitting in front of the director and he's giving me notes and each time this guy opens his mouth to talk, his dentures start to fall out of his mouth. He'd just plop'em back in and then carry on like it never happened but he would always offer me cigarettes. Like, all the darn time as if he would win a bet somewhere if I finally took one. Everyday I'd show up to set and there he was, pursing his lips around a cigarette and then pursing them again after he pulled it away so his teeth wouldn't fall out. Great guy. Great director. He died of lung cancer not too long after that and the pilot died with him. I actually met my wife on that set. We wouldn't get married until months later but that's where we met.."

"How's all that? If you don't mind me asking. I'm in my early twenties and basically live in between here at Bruce's apartment and Bruce's car so I couldn't be further from a regular or healthy home life. I'm just curious," inquired Eddie after a strong, high pause. Aubrey looked down at his candle lit lap and then around at the dark and powerless room. Submerging himself, before Eddie's eyes, into a vulnerability he hadn't felt in a long while.

"Well that makes two of us. Ya know a year or two ago, I would've said marriage has its ups and downs kid and as long as you're still willing to ride the ride together then there's no possibility that you won't enjoy the ride once it's over..." said Aubrey. Eddie didn't have the heart to admit Aubrey had accidentally drifted into a John Wayne impression mid sentence so he bit his lip.

"And now...?" asked Eddie.

Aubrey looked off out the window, maybe at that same pseudo-entity through the blinds and gulped.

"I think she's seeing someone else... Don't tell Bruce or anybody that I told you that, I don't know what it is but I trust you, kid. You're easy to talk to. I like that," he said motioning towards the closed bathroom door with Bruce humming show-tunes behind it.

"I mean, how certain are you?" asked Eddie, outside of himself.

"Well I haven't caught her with anybody yet if that's what you're asking but I'm pretty friggin' sure Eddie. It's killin' me. We tried therapy more than a few times, transcendental meditation, even a guided psilocybin therapy to try and pry out whatever negative energy we had been harboring for each other but I don't know. Something's changed..."

"You still love her?" Eddie asked.

"Of course! That's what I've been saying. I've gone through all these hoops to prove it and I mean how could I not? She was with me at my worst and stayed with me through all that and is with me now at my best. The height of this stardom and world tours and she's still by my side. I don't even know what I'd do if I found out the truth or if I saw it with my own two eyes. I just feel like something's changed... I mean shes talked me off so many ledges and stopped me from relapsing a handful of times and now I'm stressing so much about this, *that* in itself is honestly making me wanna use again," admitted Aubrey.

"Maybe you should just forget it then. Whatever you think is happening just tell yourself that you're wrong. That she's still that woman you met and bonded with and fell in love with you know? If you don't have definitive proof then you're just working yourself up over nothing," Eddie returned.

"You're pretty smart for a frickin' kid you know that? When I was your age I was drunk 23 hours of the day and high for the two hours left over. And if I wasn't doing *that* then I was chasing some young tail up and down Broadway or La Brea." Eddie sat there in the compliment all while ignoring the quality of Aubrey's math.

Just then, Bruce emerged from the bathroom with a gargantuan sigh of relief. "You know what I've never gotten a chance to tell you? You remember that one bit you had like, shit, ten years ago? Probably more but it was somethin' like——you talking to your girlfriend after she keeps yelling at you and so you say 'Listen I appreciate your ability to speak openly and honestly about your emotions but sometimes when you call me names... well people might get the wrong idea about me and their perception of me might change. Like if you call me an asshole, then everyone in town is gonna think I'm an asshole do you see what I'm saying? So my love please, I'm begging you. You gotta quit calling me cutie-pie,'" said Bruce, sending the small room back into laughter. Aubrey himself even laughed as if he had forgotten the joke entirely. Must've been the lighter's spark but he cocked his head to lean back into a memory.

"You know yeah, that was one of the first jokes that started getting around with my name attached to it. I opened for Sam Kinison with that joke. He was the final guy to tell me to go clean. He goes 'Clark it sounds fucking weird when you say *fuck* and *shit* and *ass* anyways so just don't do it! It's that simple!' Seems like so long ago now," admitted Aubrey with a decent impression. The memory now fresh beneath his skin and closer to reality than ever before. He could almost feel the goosebumps growing.

"Say, how old were you when I did that originally?" asked Aubrey. Eddie laughed.

"I'm sure I was prepubescent, but I've also been to a Gallagher show and I'm currently sitting with two fucks who are old enough to have driven drunk when it was still legal and you don't see me throwing around *that* useless information, do you?" replied Eddie. It got no laughs until Aubrey felt bad and let out a half-hearted chuckle. Suddenly Bruce lit up with excitement.

"Oh fuck, do you guys have any crazy ghost stories at the Store?" he asked. Eager for the answer, he looked out at the four eyes staring back at him blankly. "Yeah me neither," he said before deflating and then his mental train took another stop.

"Oh so what time do you wanna leave tomorrow?" he asked and then apologized for asking in front of Eddie. Earlier in the night, Aubrey mentioned having to run up

North to get a package and Bruce wound up being the driver for said expedition but they forgot to mention it to Eddie. That is, until now. Aubrey looked up from the couch and brushed it off, even inviting Eddie after regaining his breath and passing what was left of the joint to Bruce. "Eddie's a mensch! As long as he's okay with catching mono, what am I worried about? Honestly, I'd rather he just come so I don't have to talk to *you* the whole time Bruce," he said dryly. They gave him a brief rundown and upon confirmation that Eddie had no plans the next day, he joined the trip—of sorts.

"Okay look, we're going up to Santa Cruz. Santa Cruz baby! I know a guy and I left some luggage at his house and I need to go get it. So we're gonna go get it, but it'll be great. I promise. We'll see the beach. It'll be great!" Aubrey stated over his clenched pillow. The night dwindled. Placement could not be optioned properly so they lay where they fell.

MONDAY MORNING

8:00 A.M.

By six AM they had all shit, showered and shaved and hit the road in Bruce's station wagon. Squeaky-wheels and all, it rolled up the 5 towards the Grapevine. They turned off all the electronics and AC to hedge the bet that the station wagon would make it over the pass and before long Bruce was off to praising again.

"Hey Aubrey, I can't thank you enough man," stated Bruce.

"What're you thankin' me for? I said I needed to pick some stuff up from Santa Cruz and you offered to drive," returned Aubrey, nursing the seed of a headache. "Well either way I'm just happy to hangout and bullshit. I needed the vacation," Bruce claimed. He looked out onto the passing hillside and then his eyes drew down to inspect the debris along the roadside.

"Bro what the fuck do you need a vacation for? You hardly get more minutes than I do!" stated Eddie, adjusting his visor to shield the sun around the next turn.

"Hardly still counts for something doesn't it? By the way, last night? When you were out at the door? Guess who was watching my set! Go ahead, guess!" Bruce sat there, his seatbelt the only thing to contain the smugness.

"Dave Atell," he revealed. Eddie's grip on the steering wheel intensified.

"Fuck off! I saw every head who came through. I say this all the time. No he did not," proclaimed Eddie.

"Well then he must've come through the back then! Much like your mother's ex before she met your father," he prodded.

"Eat my ass Bruce! Aubrey, you know Atell. You think he was there?" asked Eddie, hoping his truth wouldn't be exposed. Aubrey looked up at the front seat and without missing a beat claimed Dave was there. Eddie's world started to crack and crumble around him.

"The fuck?!" he shouted, "Dude I'll drive us off a cliff right now. Tell me Atell wasn't there last night..." What seemed to begin as a pinch of harmless hazing turned into a harsh reality as Eddie missed crossing paths with one of his heroes.

"Yeah, he flew in with Patrice and Giraldo but in his words: 'Not on purpose,'" stated Aubrey.

"Fuck me," shouted Eddie in a defeated manor. The car was silent for more than a moment, words that should've been said weren't and words that could've been said were stirring around like the trigger finger of a gun-shy soldier. As the war of words was at a stalemate, Aubrey decided to end it.

"Pass..." he said with a tone so fitting it somehow managed to magnify the power of a single syllable word. They regained themselves from laughter and Bruce tried to piggy-back.

"Eh, I'll fuck ya Ed. As long as you like your balls blue and your glasses half empty," he said. It wasn't a very good joke but it made Eddie smile and that's what mattered.

Aubrey leaned forward in his seat, parted from the food crumbs in his lap and placed his hands on the front seats.

"Lemme ask you something. Why do you like Atell so much?" he asked hoping for some revelation of lame fandom or nerdism. It may not have been obvious but he was searching for Eddie's flaw. However, his digging only kept revealing more of Bruce.

"Can I answer that?" inserted Bruce, "He's honest. Even when he's full of shit he's being honest. He doesn't need to knock, he kicks in the door and that's why I'll never be a household name and he is..." Amongst that sulking, Eddie was processing his friend, a world of emotions all in the passenger seat. "Jesus Bruce," intercepted Aubrey, "You gotta stop beating yourself up like that. Between your words and both palms you'll have no confidence and even less skin on your junk by the time we even get there. I invited-" Aubrey stopped and corrected himself,

"I wanted to drive with you because I see potential in you, if you can hone it! I've seen you do great and you don't give yourself enough credit…" It was in that moment, that is if they hadn't realized it already that *this* was the benefit to Bruce and Eddie taking the trip with Aubrey. Professional life lessons aren't always learned in a classroom setting but out in the field, with the pain and memories of your mistakes under your feet making sure you take that next step, especially if you're flat footed.

See the thing Aubrey couldn't quite put to words is that writing and a quick whit may be the most powerful tool in a comic's arsenal but just as important are the two M's. The miles and the minutes. He explained to them the difference between being funny on one coast opposed to the other or up in the mountains and how a topical reference of geography can overpower and influence the demographic at any moment, if done right. To a layman it would come off as gibberish but both Eddie and Bruce were taking mental notes.

Another mile passed and Eddie got the guts to ask his last question about Atell.

"Did you at least talk to him? What'd you say? What'd *he* say?" asked Eddie almost urgently.

"I got off stage and we just chatted about the crowd. I told him what you and I usually talk about Aubrey. Learning to know when to walk away. Ya know, getting to know when to leave while you're ahead but he leans in and goes: 'I disagree—I can say with honesty it is never too late to off yourself in a pinch,'" repeated Bruce looking over at

Eddie smiling from ear to ear. Bruce was laughing his ass off at "*In a pinch*" when he looked back at Aubrey in the back seat. He was smiling but for some reason his eyes weren't along for the ride..

10:58 A.M.

Eddie veered left in Lost Hills headed towards Paso Robles. The history buff Bruce ordered them to pull over at the crash site of James Dean. The car labored across the dusty gravel lot, striking up sticks and pebbles in it's path and came to a screeching halt upon contact with a dilapidated concrete block. The faded air-freshener jolted forward making contact with the windshield and swung like a pendulum. It's swinging signified the approaching reality of the moment's task and it wasn't the pee break. The three men took a breath and stepped out into the thick summer air of Cholame, California. It was hot but closer to hell. They left the car to bake and walked by the "Beware of Rattlesnakes" sign to sit down next to the big lonely tree. It's shade humbling, giving back life to the weary travelers under the unforgiving sun and its 112 degree heat. Every so often a small gust of wind would pass through the gravel lot as cars whirred by but it made no difference as it had already picked up the heat from the road.

"This is what's called a Tree of Heaven. I can't tell you the real name because I don't speak Latin," said Bruce looking up at the tree.

"You don't?" joked Eddie, as if a deity just admitted a flaw.

"Fuck off," jabbed Bruce before continuing, "In 1955 James Dean crashed here. Well not here-here but just up the road a bit. And when I was a kid they planted this tree here as a memorial. I remember reading about it."

"No shit?" said Aubrey as he looked around and seemed to take in the moment.

"Yeah... he died and all that greatness died with'em," stated Bruce as if he himself was giving the eulogy. As noon approached, they felt best to just leave Bruce's emotional hornets nest alone. They could feel the scorching sun crawl across the sky but the shade of that big heavenly tree left them in Eden amongst the tall grass and roasting soil.

"What are we doin' this for again?" asked Eddie, looking out through the waves of heat on the golden hills. Droplets of sweat infested his scalp before beaming down his temples leaving Eddie's skin crawling.

Aubrey hadn't taken a turn driving yet, his eyes were twice as low as both Eddie and Bruce, he took a bite down on a piece of straw and seemed to look inside himself. "We're going to Santa Cruz. Santa Cruz baby! I know a guy and I left some luggage at his house and I need to go get it. So we're gonna go get it, but it'll be great. I promise. We'll see the beach. We'll get some food, see some ass. You can get a drink," Bruce wiped the sweat from his own brow and grabbed the straw. His explanation was about the same as the first time Eddie asked but this time there seemed to be less vigor in his answer as if his own enthusiasm for the trip was draining.

"We should get outta here. Not because I'm sweating through my pants but because I recognize a few of these haircuts and they don't mess around. I know that asymmetrical bob anywhere. Let's get going," quipped Aubrey, also noticing a few folks he assumed would recognize him.

They filed back into the car and hesitated to touch the scalding seatbelts. The smell of hot stagnant air encapsulated them in a furnace and for a brief second they considered getting back out of the car. Maybe it was the glare of the windshield or the blinding reflective light off the weathered dash but it all screamed retreat.

1:16 P.M.

About two hours after pulling out of that gravel lot and rolling down the simmering, double golden-line divided pavement did they pass through Watsonville and then Santa Cruz proper. They took the fishhook up to Mission, passed Swift Street and out towards Davenport.

"I thought you said we were going to Santa Cruz," said Bruce after Eddie read aloud the MapQuest directions that Aubrey had printed out earlier.

"Well he's actually in Bonny Doon (my friend). So we'll go there first and then grab some food at the beach and head back that cool?" stated Aubrey. The boys confirmed with a side-eye caught on the rear view mirror.

After a fifteen minute windy swell through the mountains they pulled into the dirt driveway of Aubrey's friend Clay. That was all he said, Aubrey that is. The man he called Clay stepped out of his tiny house and shook Aubrey's hand. There were goats and dogs roaming the yard and the biggest Maine Coon cat a man has ever seen sat motionless on the front porch like an Egyptian guardian. Eddie and Bruce decided that the cat was truly the owner of that tiny house. Clay may think he owns the place but that cat was in charge. They watched as Aubrey and Clay exchanged greetings only to then exchange something with the other hand. They hugged and then Clay took Aubrey over to the garage with the dogs in toe. The goats however, remained. Four or five of them looked up from their grassy post with mouths gyrating in chew, their horizontal eyes dead set on Eddie and Bruce sitting in their driveway.

"I don't like this man. Where'd they go and why are they looking at us like that?" sheepishly asked Bruce.

"I don't know I kinda like it," said Eddie, his jaw now began moving in the same rotation. Mimicking the chewing motion. Bruce begged him to stop and started to open the door but the moment he did the shriek of a goat rang out into the afternoon air. Bruce slammed the door shut and swatted away at what he thought was a fly. All the while, Eddie chewed along with his hoofed compadres. Two hours went by before Bruce's head popped up.

"Oh thank god!" shouted Bruce as Aubrey emerged behind a truck and came back down the driveway with two suitcases that looked bigger than they were heavy. He put them in the back of the station wagon, got in and didn't say a word other than, "Let's eat."

The old wagon started up again and they drove back down that winding Bonny Doon road and then along the 1, their radio crashing out as the signal got lost along the roaming Monterey Bay coastline. That is until hitting the many lights of Mission street. They dragged on fatigued and dug down the hill into downtown Santa Cruz for a piece of pizza and a drink at The Red Room. The type of dive bar that dove with it's eyes closed and hit the concrete hard. Eddie and Aubrey were trying to hype Bruce up to go talk to a girl at the other end of the bar. They sat under the red lights of the bar as if it were the engine room of a submarine.

"Ya know every once in a while a six trips over itself and winds up standing in line as a nine and nones the wiser, who's to say you can't fool'em?" joked Aubrey. Bruce was too drunk to follow along but smiled, yelled okay and walked off towards the other end of the bar. Aubrey motioned for the bartender and ordered another drink for Eddie.

"Can I ask you something? And I'd appreciate if you answered honestly," asked Aubrey with a tone that was starting to become normal to Eddie.

"Of course," he responded. Aubrey took a big breath and then took a modest sip of his sparkling Diet Coke on ice.

"Do you think I have a problem?" he asked. Eddie looked Aubrey up and down a bit and said, "Problem with what? It's only a Diet Coke." Aubrey looked around the bar and gazed at all the bobbing heads and smiling faces.

"Look, California sober sounds cool at parties but I'm starting to smoke like Popeye needs spinach and I'm running outta cans..." Aubrey admitted with another guilty glance around the bar and for the first time ever, Eddie Mason looked eye to eye with one of his idols. Not as a star or a business man or the courts' jester but as a human being. He reverberated Aubrey's words inside himself for as long as he could before common decency required an answer.

"I feel that. But can I tell you somethin'? Sometimes the *can* itself can give you that—I mean, you think Popeye never had a big can of spinach on him and knew he had that Ace up his sleeve?" asked Eddie before continuing in philosophizing Popeye the Sailor, "I may be out of hand but if you think about it, sometimes possession fulfills the need of gluttony just by access. You can be the guy who can but doesn't. If you're strong enough..."

"I don't know if I can do that man," replied Aubrey without much reflection. "If you're close enough to opening the book you have to be open enough to close it too. Think about that, I gotta take a piss," stated Eddie. He stepped away and Bruce walked back with a number and an even bigger smile.

5:02 P.M.

Eddie came back, they finished their drinks and Aubrey then directed them out to the Boardwalk and they felt the sand on their feet. It had been a long time for Bruce, specifically because he was raised in a landlocked state for most of his life and then never stopped working. They had enough time to think to themselves before a final pass along West Cliff Drive then headed back. This time, Eddie drove like he was trying to beat rush hour in LA and they were back in no time, all the while both him and Bruce asking what was in those bags. Aubrey avoided the question but presented a joint. It was thicker than the one Bruce had brought so excitement filled the cab. They sparked up while Aubrey took a nap. Both Eddie and Bruce looked off into the dark distance and wished a higher speed was allowed. Bruce noticed Eddie's falling eyelids and offered to take the rest of the drive so they switched places at the next rest stop and Eddie passed out in the passenger seat.

Soon they were pulling back into Bruce's parking spot in Burbank. Aubrey used Bruce's phone and called for a ride home. He kicked back with them for another fifteen minutes and shot the shit before whooshing off in an SUV with both of his bags. The night was far from over yet Eddie and Bruce were both too exhausted to even get dinner. They jumped into better sleeping positions than car seats and crashed until dawn broke.

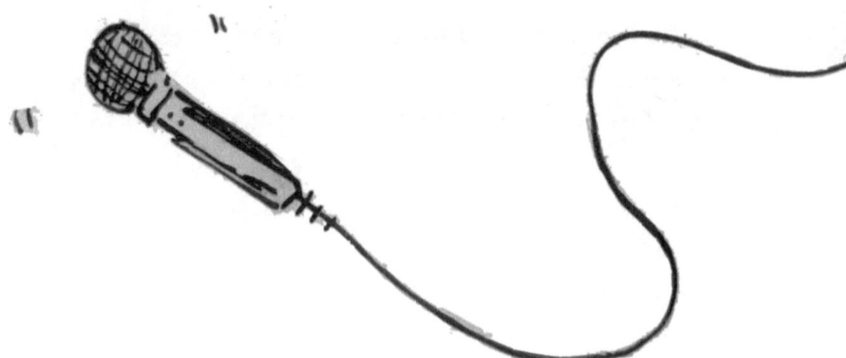

TUESDAY AFTERNOON

2:34 P.M.

Eddie sat on the couch with nothing to watch on TV and Bruce fast asleep beside him. His angst increasing almost as quick as his boredom, he stood up and retrieved a Walkman from the cabinet beneath the TV, then found some headphones. Eddie changed into shorts and pushed a cassette into the player after inserting the headphone jack. He went downstairs and stretched on the sidewalk to prepare for a late day run. Cars whizzed by and buses burped as they pushed through the nearest intersection.

As soon as Eddie took his first step he looked down to press play on the cassette, *Moonshake* by CAN started resonating through the faded foam covering of the headphones.

The beat continued to set his pace as he crossed a side street and ran for a couple blocks down Magnolia Blvd before he cut up to West Burbank Blvd where he was brought to a halt. As he caught his heavy breath he looked around from the corner at all the cars stopped at the intersection. The power must've gone out leaving all the traffic lights flashing red for every direction. Reasonably heavy traffic congested the intersection while Eddie waited for his moment to chance a turn through untrustworthy vehicles like a kid prepares to jump into a double-dutch. That moment appeared, Eddie looked in all directions and then lightly jogged across the street with clear right of way.

All of a sudden a car came to a screeching halt narrowly missing him in the crosswalk as it lurched forward. Thankfully Eddie dodged the front bumper because his feet were already moving but it was beyond close. The woman driving covered her mouth in shock and hit her breaks so hard that she was almost rear ended by the truck behind her. The truck's horn rang out like a ship approaching port. The man stuck his head and arm out of the window and screamed obscenities just before Eddie pulled off his headphones to address the narrowly avoided catastrophe.

The lady in the front car rolled her window down in an apologetic panic. She asked Eddie if he was alright and he was. She asked if he was hurt in any way or if she actually hit him and she didn't so he wasn't. She explained that she was trying to get to Victory Blvd but was lost before wiping what looked like a tear from her eye and went on about a family emergency.

"Looking for victory...aren't we all..." Eddie thought then politely told her she was going the wrong direction but to go all the way down the other way, it will vier left and you'll hit Victory in a few streets. Just keep your eyes out and you'll see it he said. Eddie felt like Aubrey must feel telling openers at the Store which way they needed to go or what to do to make it. Then again there is something cathartic about successfully giving someone directions when you know exactly where or what they are looking for. Like a wise man of the sun scorched land, deep in the valley of Tongva territory aiding a weary or lost traveller.

She fought back her swelling tears and quickly whipped the car around in the intersection proving her urgency and burned rubber down Burbank in the direction Eddie directed. He finished crossing the street and put the headphones back on then continued his trot down the sidewalk. He decided to run all the way to Victory. If that lady didn't make it...he would.

Many green street signs passed above him before his warn shoes set down on the corner of Burbank and Victory. Eddie smiled, he thought about reaching this victorious touchstone yet also that the journey wasn't over, the arduous trek all the way back to Bruce's was in front of him. Then his mind wandered to why Bruce was so fucking dramatic and such a drain, on both emotions and attention? And why Aubrey was so cagey during the trip up to Santa Cruz. What was that about? Who the hell was that Clay guy? What's his deal? Some random civilian living out in the woods near the cliffed beaches with a barnyard for a garden, yet he knows Aubrey Clark well enough to have him drive 5 hours for some questionable luggage? What the actual fuck was in those bags? Was it drugs? Was Aubrey planning on using again? He said he was smoking a bunch of pot but was that so bad?

Then with his hands on his hips in a slow moving stride back down Burbank Eddie clasped his hands atop his head for breath and drifted back into thought.

Would reaching success as a comic come as easily or as fluently as this run? Not that it was easy but he was five miles in and on his way back from Victory with his head held high and a grin from the tunes providing his soundtrack. Surely stardom was harder to reach than a Boulevard in the San Fernando Valley sun but speaking of Shirley...

What about that hysteric woman? Was she alright? Had she ever made it to the emergency let alone the Boulevard?

The sun's rays beamed down on him and as the heat reacted to his sweat a singe shot down his spine as if it were ice upon his skin. That tingle was his known signal of the pinnacle, that marker during a run where your exhaustion and total fatigue turns into a bullrush of adrenaline and the wind returns to your lungs like a gust from an approaching storm over an unforgiving ocean. With his engine turning Eddie pushed on with an ambitious pace and he made it home before his sweating stopped to signify dehydration. Eddie walked to the kitchen sink to pour himself a cup of water, on the way there he passed the open bathroom door. Eddie's head and neck swooped back into the doorway like a cartoon to see Bruce standing in the shower, it's see-through plastic curtain shading nothing from sight since the doorway was all the way open. Bruce stood there with his hand up against the pseudo-masonry wall and stared into the steaming shower head. There's no way of knowing how long he had been in there but the bathroom mirror was fogged up like a horror flick.

"Better than taking a bath, that's what killed rock and roll," Eddie thought and then ran to the kitchen counter to write down the thought onto a lined yellow pad. He poured himself a cup of water which reminded him of the poor plumbing. By the time the cup was full a terrorizing scream blared out from the shower, echoing off fake tile to ricochet sound out of the bathroom door like a cannon. Eddie hopped over to the sauna door realizing he cut off Bruce's hot water.

"My bad dude, I forgot!" shouted Eddie over the sound of the stream of water.

"Fuck that's cold! Fuck!" shouted back Bruce holding himself away from the water as it slowly warmed back up.

"But whenever you're done playing with yourself I gotta take a shower, I went for a run to clear my head. I almost got hit by a car—it was great." Eddie said leaning against the doorway and clearly still catching his breath.

All of a sudden Bruce stuck his head out of the shower shielding himself with the curtain.

"Woah dude are you okay?" he asked with both hands clenched in plastic. Eddie confirmed he was fine, just had a good run and had a lot on his mind and needed a shower. Bruce reached over to the water and tested for heat. He then explained that whatever they drank had given him a head-crushing headache and he needed another minute. Eddie shook his head.

"Dude why are you even covering yourself I can see everything!" shouted Eddie staring down at Bruce's body through the clear curtain. Bruce looked down at himself still holding the curtain up for decency just above the nipples with both hands.

"Oh yeah," he said with an embarrassed smile, "Just give me like two more minutes," he finished. Eddie rolled his eyes and obliged only to find himself quenching for another cup of water. He neglected the urges hoping to honor Bruce's two minutes and decided to stretch. His legs were so sore the burn as he bent down was like an incendiary going off. He spread his legs and leaned to his left and then his right for what felt like an eternity. The fiery sensation dimmed and he pulled each ankle up behind him to stretch his quads. He looked over at the pen and pad on the counter and reached for it. He stopped stretching and wrote down:

"When rockstars go to rehab why not say 'Do all the drugs you want. Just not in a bathtub.'

Too many lost, too many lost." Eddie smiled and set

the pad back down before placing his shoes over by the door and then sitting down on the couch. His sweat still cold as it pressed up against the couch. More time passed and Eddie started to get hungry. He pulled a pan out and set it on the stove before walking towards the bathroom door. The hot shower still running, Eddie pushed into the doorway to a frightful surprise.

"Hey Bruce do you want any eggs? Oh damn come-on! My bad but come-on!" he asked and shouted. Bruce rushed to cover himself with his hands and deny then very quickly just apologized but Eddie had already retreated.

When Bruce was finally finished and the water turned off, he stepped out of the bathroom with a towel wrapped around his head as if he had long wet hair and then another towel tucked around his body just above the nipples. He knew what he was doing...

"Although I may have just been violated by an intruder in my own home—I am finished with the private bathing facility and it is now your turn..." he said backing away from Eddie like a victim as he passed. Eddie shook his head and smiled with a fresh towel under his arm before placing it on the rack below the bathroom's miniature window. He closed the door for privacy and then opened the window to let the musk out. The window's seal was tough and took effort to pry apart implying Bruce's neglect for fresh air.

He looked out that tiny window and across the small balconies next door to admire the sky beyond. The sun seemed to be setting early and pushed a mirage of pink and orange clouds across the dull blue sky. He turned the water on as hot as it would get and rinsed the shower before stepping in and taking what amounted to a five minute cold shower.

7:00 P.M.

The next day they were at the Store again and even earlier than the other night. Bruce and Eddie showed up before sundown after deciding to walk the strip and smoke one of the joints Aubrey left them. An almost unnoticed entrance turned into paradise as they were greeted like knights after reaching the green room.

"Excuse me, if it isn't the two bums of Burbank. My favorite henchmen... B and E!" shouted Aubrey over the room. The two entered almost clueless to a room of: Aubrey, Penny, Genie, Gilda and Karl.

"I knew Bruce was an asshole but I didn't know he conned Eddie unto the dark side," touted Karl with a Star Wars reference.

"Oh too soon! Too soon! That bastard of a movie came out like two years ago. That wound is still very raw. It was barely even Star Wars and depicted something else entirely," joked Penny, her cadence perfect as always and referring to the prequel to the Star Wars Trilogy.

"It wasn't that bad, Jesus! I watched it with my kid and he loved it. If it's silly enough for him then I'm sold on account of him being my spawn. If not then my name's not Pam Santiago." stated "Genie" Santiago. Gilda Bean had had enough.

"What the fuck are we talkin' about here? What is this the review?" shouted Gilda with the same dry humor that had worked for nearly thirty years. She made close to half a million dollars (American) on t-shirts alone with her slogan on it and that doesn't count the random raunchy ad placements. Almost fifteen years ago, in 1987, Gilda walked up on stage with damn near a mullet and a Canadian Tuxedo and said:

"You ever have coke dick..? It's like whiskey dick but with diet soda." And killed. For whatever reason a woman that looked and acted like her worked, and she was thrown into the spotlight. Coming from a small town she never went too far from her roots in the sense that The Comedy Store was where she grew up in her career and she never wanted to leave that. That's how Eddie wanted to be and one of his only plans was to never leave the Store. Just like Bobby Lee, Penny Peterson, Genie Santiago, Aubrey Clark and I guess Karl Phan, in a way. They found stardom but never left the hub of what got them there; the Store. Everyone calmed back down after Gilda's rile up. Bobby finished his drink and ran his palms across his newly buzzed head.

"What's the craziest thing you've ever said on stage? Please, I need to know," claimed Bobby with a devious smile. He caught the room in a lull and stole the attention.

"Well I've never taken my pants off that's for sure," stated Aubrey. Penny burst out laughing followed by Genie and Bruce. All except for Gilda, she seemed to drink her drink as if nothing had been said.

"You're obviously excluded, you're a legend but... you'll say anything..." said Bobby. She smiled and took another sip. Her eyes told a world of stories all in a moment as they shot off under the dim light. Suddenly the room lit up and in walked Leland Poe. His glistening eyes crossed the room before legs could allow.

"Is that fucking lipstick?" shouted Penny at the red kiss mark on Leland's neck. He immediately started rubbing his face and neck.

"I can't get-any yet this son of a bitch has to fight women off stage just to finish his set," said Karl.

"You may not be able to pull a lady but you can write a fuckin' joke I'll give ya that," said Genie with a raspy laugh and candid support.

"Okay but can we answer the fucking question? I'm sorry, not everything is about a pretty white boy with a razor sharp jawline. I'd fuck him too but I'm just saying, c'mon can we answer the question?" shouted Bobby in a fit.

"Yeah I wanna hear Aubrey too. Let's see what you've got Mr. TV Dad," said Penny who in no way kept her mouth closed when it came to curse words. They all turned towards Aubrey hoping to hear to raunchiest thing he had ever said on stage. Circling him like flies on a corpse.

"In a minute Bob, you got anything new tonight kid?" Aubrey asked Leland as he grabbed a water bottle and took a few sips, swatting away the flies surrounding him. Genie saw the deflection and filled the silence.

"Sorry Bobby but I miss the time when I was coming

up and Gilda was our barometer of hedonism. Gilda I was in the audience when I was seventeen with my girlfriends when you came out on stage, not literally, but we were drunk as hell but still I'll never forget it. You said:

'You know I was walking along the train tracks one day when I remembered a friend of mine was going to school to become an Engineer. He told me that only 2 graduating classes each year have a woman in them, which means that most if not all train conductors are male. If that's true then why is it that every woman I meet says they wanna run a train? What is it? What is this hypocritical bullshit? That same secret desire transcending to multiple women...

I can't afford a therapist! Who am I supposed to talk about this to...?'"

The room cracked up except for Aubrey and Leland, still locked in, who replied and his confidence filled the room amongst scattered feelings. He heard his name announced and stepped out through the curtain and onto the stage. After a slow introduction he sat down on the stool and looked around for a while. Then to the front row where a large gentleman was sitting with a giant tattoo on his arm. Leland looked down and said,

"Jesus! How many swastikas is *that* a cover-up of?" And went from there.

9:05 P.M.

Back in the green room Gilda was finishing her thought in return,

"You had your gold too without going blue. You said, 'My name is Pam but they always called me Genie after my mom's friend from Frisco in the 70's. They called her Genie the Hook and it wasn't cuz she fished...'"

Suddenly Bruce, remembering the bit with nostalgia finished that final bit with:

"'Great gal!'" laughing with his eyes set on Genie and waiting to meet her reciprocating gaze. The room released but not after a few of the comics took a moment to bash Leland. Genie and Gilda agreed, he was a cocky little twerp with no real talent. "He's only gotten as far as he has because of his looks!" added Bruce with an air of irritability about him. Eddie didn't really say much but Penny added that she thought he was nice around her but a creep around others. Finally, Aubrey decided to speak up in defense. "Somebody's gotta say *something* positive. Come on guys we're peers here aren't we? Lee's a great kid and I believe in him and at the end of the day, is he funny or not? Exactly!" shouted Aubrey, managing to be the only one to ever stick up for him. Just then, Leland's set ended and he reentered the green room without really looking around at anyone. Genie thought that strange. Bruce finished his drink and asked Eddie if he wanted a refill. Eddie obliged and saw off his empty glass in the arms of Latto. Bruce walked through the curtain and put away the empty glasses neglecting refills and then quickly made his way to the stage for his allotted time. He scrunched his nose and said,

"You guys believe in ghosts? I went to a bed and breakfast recently and it was haunted. Before I went, all my friends kept calling me and warning me like:

'Aren't you worried a ghost will get you while you're sleeping?' and I said sleeping?! I'm here for breakfast!" Bruce exhaled as the crowd looked over at each other smiling.

"I think a panda looks like a sober koala who just embraced food as their new passion. 'Cuz Koalas are little itty-bitty creatures that cling to branches but really they're hardcore fiends. Twenty-hour sleep schedule with a four hour devour window, and in that window they mostly eat Eucalyptus which is poison. Buzzed on demon-root juice until they fall out of forty foot trees only to pop back up like nothing happened and then look at you funny. That means when you see a Koala in person or on TV and they have that pleasant little smile? Thats not obedience, thats not acting. They're high! They are high!! Just sit around and getting rowdy because they're sleep deprived little bitches disguised as a teddybear...

Meanwhile Pandas are chill and calm but the size of a human being.

'We eat clean and only clean! Have you had bamboo? It's great!!'

But they never stop eating. They still show those scars of addiction and carnage, the dark circles under their innocent eyes and the body bruising.

'I was once like you——thin, small, funny-lookin and riddled with chlamydia. Now I'm big, healthy and roll around for fun. Sometimes I fall off branches because I sneezed, I'm so silly!'

But hey, don't let the pot belly fool you, I'm no expert on either of them... I'm just sayin." The crowd sat in silence and a man cleared his throat in the far back.

10:15 P.M.

In the green room:

"Poe! There's a lot of experience back here, do you want any notes?" she asked with the tone of a loaded gun. He looked up from a magazine and gave a false smile and said "What? No I'm okay." Penny put her head down and shook it.

"Dude," she said silently to herself.

"Eddie. Tell me a joke. Now! Go," yelled Penny in a playful manner. Eddie didn't even clear his throat:

"What do you call a braindead pickle with no arms or legs?" he asked. The room sat in bewilderment.

"What?" they all responded in unison.

"A vegetable," Eddie replied.

"Screw you man!" shouted Aubrey trying hard to hide his smile in the corn-infested-air.

"Okay, okay, okay. What do you call an old person you can't get rid of?" he asked. Everyone chuckled and Penny was already smiling.

"What?" she asked with delight.

"A boomerang," said Eddie. No smile, no recognition just riding the joke. Aubrey calmed his laughter only to ask if he could use that on stage. Then he half-jokingly proposed that he give a set up and Eddie give the answer. If Eddie's answer was any good Aubrey said he would try it on stage. A big opportunity disguised as play. Then, thinking off the top of his head, Aubrey spilled out:

"Okay, what do you call a... rabid dog that's foaming at the mouth with no leash... but no legs?" He barely finished the sentence before shaking with laughter and without a beat Eddie said,

"You don't... its not goin' anywhere." Aubrey crumbled, actually rolling on the floor in hysterics, along with everyone else. The whole green room seemed to shake in tears and the audience never heard a damn thing. Aubrey pushed out his hand to shake with a heavy smile. Eddie spit in his hand and then shook it sending Aubrey bursting back into laughter, trying to pull his hand away from Eddie. It got a laugh though.

Eddie smiled and let go just before "*Bruce Latto!*" was heard over the speakers and Bruce walked back in and sat on the couch in a huff.

"I fucking suck. I fucking suck," he repeated. Gilda rearranged herself in her seat and said, "You don't suck Bruce. *That* sucked, but you don't suck." Wise words if you're mature enough to handle them. Gilda stood up and walked towards the door and said, "See ya pussies!" "*Gilda Bean everybody!*" shouted the MC over the house speakers. Gilda walked on stage, her hips giving the same gusto as an old Buick and everyone in the building seemed to be paying attention. After reaching center-stage she did an entire bit of sniffing the microphone for a smell which lead to her hands and then the audience before sniffing her own armpit and walking back on stage.

"Before I start I'd like to tell everyone to tip your servers and treat them better. I worked in the service industry for years and I'll tell you what, it's misleading as hell. Not everything is what it seems so don't let'em fool ya!

Think about the *SPECIALS*! YOU may think its special because it's not normally on the menu, but the only reason for that is cuz it sucks to make, and we're too tired to make it all the god damned time so until that special day, you're gonna get the same easy-to-make slop we normally dish out.

Now think about *HAPPY HOUR*! YOU might be happy, but don't let the fake smiles fool ya champ! Every single person behind that bar is fighting themselves trying not to kill you. Don't even start with a wedge salad. What is a wedge salad?!

As a kid my mom bought two heads of lettuce and that was the dinner for the six of us. That's it! And now you want me to pay more, to do more, while you do less? That's a tough sell sister...do you got any specials?

By the way, since when is it so expensive to park a fucking car outside of the place you work. I took my anger out on a few nice ones on the way in so, let's all be nicer to each other, and if when the shows over you find out it was *you* that got your car scratched then congratulations... and my condolences."

12:01 A.M.

Back in the green room, they were talking about best cigarette brands. Aubrey hadn't put one to his lips in four months but indulged in the topic. He was soaking it all in. They went through every one and went off on the mascots for each.

"I swear though it's already changed in just a few months. What's a pack at now?" asked Aubrey.

"These were two twenty-five," said Genie, holding up the pack from her pocket.

"I don't *smoke-smoke* but the last time I bought cigarettes they were under two bucks, if this keeps up I'll either not be able to afford them or I guess I'll start doing terrible and disgusting things to get what I want," stated Penny like a bunny with a knife.

"If there's one thing I can tell you honestly that I miss it's that rush of menthol," admitted Aubrey once more. The room agreed.

"Wait so you don't miss drinkin'?" asked Bruce cheekily. Aubrey smiled and then seemingly re-asked himself the question.

"I miss the camaraderie that accompanies drinking and at times I do miss just having a little buzz yeah, but what I do not miss is the next day and then what usually happens to me the few days, weeks, months after." Aubrey trailed off to release a silent burp.

"That's my dad!" shouted Penny like a child actor. Just then, the MC popped their head in to quiet the couches.

"Hey! The laughs are supposed to be coming from out here guys. Keep it down!" they shouted in a whisper. That only rolled the room over more.

"Oh, fuck! Eddie you're up next! What are you doing dude?" shouted Penny, startled. Eddie nonchalantly replied,

"Nah, I didn't know Aubrey was going to show up so I gave him my set instead of getting bumped."

"WHAT?!" exclaimed Penny and Genie in a frantic unison.

"What? It's just minutes P. It'll be okay, he's only in town for like a week and a half," he replied. Penny sat up.

"Dude! Genie, Gilda and I spoke up for you man. We got you that spot. Pass or fail, it's on you but we put in for you. I didn't wanna say that in front of everybody but... fuck. This is a big opportunity for you. Fucking *was...*" she taunted before finally taking a stand.

"Sorry, I'm pissed. I'm not gonna go out there now and you, you're taking my spot. Bitch! How do you like them apples, Edward?" she asked childishly. They were both now standing but Mr. Clark stood up.

"Hey, guys. I never meant to steal, or bump, or pry, or take advantage. I like Eddie a lot, and I think he is just as amazing as you do and I haven't even known him for what three days? I showed up to say what's up and he offered.

I took it as a gesture. We've spent a whole friggin' car ride together and I didn't even pretend to hop in the driver's seat so the least I can do is... ya know—" he was cut off by Gilda Bean's exit from the stage.

"Special guest, Aubrey Clark everybody! Let's roll!!!" shouted the MC. The room practically blew up with definite fatigue to every loose hinge or tipped chair in the building. Aubrey took the stage with shine.

"Thank you! Thank you! Before I accept this award, humbly. I'd like to start with a joke..." Aubrey said before standing still. After a moment, he looked down at himself then back at the crowd and said "Why aren't you laughing?" Making fun of his current appearance. The crowd started laughing but before they could take another breath, Aubrey dove in.

"Come on! I put all this work in to a joke and I dress up like a clown and show up and look at me!" He shouted at the few who hadn't already broken.

"Well fine! Uuugh! I'll stoop down to your level!" he shouted now and leapt into the crowd and onto the lap of a patron sitting in the front row.

"What do you call a forty-two year old man that you can't get rid of?" he said while seated on her lap. The crowd smiled in amusement, not knowing whether to reply or not.

"A boomerang!" he shouted before pretending to throw such a device and jumping off her lap and then coming right back.

Pretending to be a flying object really takes a toll, he

cleared his throat and caught his breath while the crowd threw themselves at him with laughter.

"Ma'am, you right there. What do you call a rabid dog who's foaming at the mouth with no leash but no legs?" he asked with a faux-sad face and a fake tear in his eye. His eyes ran across glazed pupils and shaking heads so he cut the cord.

"Not my problem——idiot," he said casually. That practically blew the roof off the place and placed it back where it was supposed to be. Aubrey said it so matter-of-factly you'd think he came up with it himself. Regardless of who penned it, he knew how to rope up a room. Random folks were high-fiving and smiling to the person on either side of them.

Back in the green room:

"Eddie what the fuck man! Are you trying to just sabotage your own career? I can't believe you!" shouted Penny in Eddie's face. Gilda and Genie joined in the berating as Bruce watched in amusement only to distract himself from the sadness of his own set. One or two other comics sat in the corner uncomfortable but also ready if a spot-filler was needed in the most comical way. Eddie decided to stand up for himself after being told to.

"Hey! It's my life and it's Aubrey fucking Clark are you out of your mind?" he shouted.

"So the fuck what kid?! We put our necks out for you!" shouted Gilda.

"Yeah!!" shouted Genie. Penny grabbed him by the shoulders and forced him to look her in the eyes. "Eddie. I know we're friends... but I will kick your fuckin' ass if you don't take my spot. So help me god! Its literally the headlining spot, jesus christ!" she shouted before raising her clenched fist to punch—no one believed her.

"Fine I'll do it. But not because you're holding me hostage or anything, I'm doing it because you're literally holding me hostage. I want to go home now. I'm eh-scared," Eddie murmured sarcastically. Suddenly, the MC popped through the curtain.

"What the fuck are we doing? Who am I announcing? Penny you told me you'd fucking come right back!" they shouted.

"Hey! Fuck you dude! This is a real conflict we're having here and I don't need your matrix looking ass to keep hopping on my neck okay? Is that okay with you, Mr. Anderson?" Penny said in a way that's best to be forgotten.

"Fuck me, alright—me," stated Eddie matter-of-factly. The MC cursed them out one last time before purposefully then putting on their *smiling-clown-crowd-face* in front of everyone and storming off and just then, over the loud speakers came,

"Let's hear it for Aubrey Clark!!! Thank you so much for coming through brotha. And for our headliner tonight! The one! The only! EDDIEEE MASON!!"

"I'm tired of defending my out of date news feed. Like, let's be real I'm a comic I can't afford to keep buying the paper...

I get my news from the lady that lives in that van outside the Ralph's on Sherman Way. Which is fine it's just, if there's ever a major catastrophe... I'm in real trouble..." he waded through the choppy waters until reaching his closing joke.

"I just got out of a relationship... like six years ago. It was so toxic. She lost her *B* over time and then the town forced her to surrender her *W* and now... she was just an *itch*—but it had transcended the two of us and our friends started to take notice. One day my friend pulled me aside and asked what was going on and I said,

'I had two options: I can break up with her clean, like a man.' My buddy looked at me and asked what the other option was? I looked back at him and said,

Well I can't kill'er—she'd take too long to get ready."

1:56 A.M.

Eddie Mason walked offstage to a tremendous applause from his peers and with matching feedback from some of the folks nearest him.. The sentiment didn't go unnoticed as he looked off into the neon-soaked crowd showing their love in a way he hadn't quite felt before. Unbeknownst to Eddie, a woman slipped right past him and headed towards the green room to introduce herself to Aubrey. Said woman was the lead talent-scout for The Late Late

Show with Craig Kilborn. She introduced herself and pulled Aubrey off to the side. They spoke for no less than ten minutes before exchanging contact information, shaking hands and then the talent scout sent Eddie a stare across the sea of turning heads on her way out. That stare shook Eddie to his core, he couldn't rationalize a decent explanation. Was it bad? Was it good? Who the fuck even was that? Did she recognize me?

"Yeah hi, I was just on stage," Eddie stammered to himself.

The crowd cleared and the talent reconvened to chat it up. They gave each other praise and Eddie confronted Penny to apologize. Before she separated from their hug she turned her head and whispered into Eddie's ear:

"Joke's on you. Aubrey Clark just opened for you... bitch!" Then walked away without effort or flaw. She was a phoenix coasting through the ember encrusted air of the Comedy Store. It may not have been by design but you can be damn sure it was still true, sorta. Suddenly Eddie felt a stiff hand across his back. It was Bruce.

"Hey bud. I know things are still goin' here but Aubrey wants to kick it outside by the cars real quick. Come on," he said discreetly while sipping his beer. The back lot was vacant except for a security guard off to the side and then there was Aubrey, leaning up against the tail-end of Bruce's station wagon. He was chewing on a straw or whatever was left of it before retracting it to speak.

"Hey kiddo. Got some good news, I figured we should celebrate," he said removing a fat joint from his breast pocket, then a lighter. Bruce grinned like a schoolboy as Eddie placed his unfinished drink on top of the car above the window with writing. With its tantalizingly filthy patina and aura of dust, dirt and grime the station wagon had become a billboard for people's thoughts. The window below Eddie's drink read:

LOVE

~~CLEAN~~ ME ALONE

LEAVE

Eddie smiled, "I'm always down to smoke, especially if it's your grass, man. What's the good news?" he asked in a winding trail of thought. The flick of the lighter rang out into the moonlight. Under that moonlight fanned a small, cupped flame held in front of and slowly approaching the joint's fat end. The heat singed the tip before quickly engulfing it in a micro-explosion. Aubrey blew it out with ease and took a long deserving drag. Eddie watched and could only speculate as to what Aubrey imagined he was truly smoking. "Survey says, somethin' else," thought Eddie silently to himself. Aubrey passed it to an eager Bruce, and then placed his palm on Bruce's shoulder. "There was a talent scout in the crowd tonight, we talked, and they want me to do the Late Late show in a few days. Craig had a decent role in the movie we just did so it's not outta left field but I'll be honest, I haven't done that one yet so this is a big deal to me. I need to bring some heat and whoever I bring with needs to too," he said. Aubrey had formed a reputation over the years for having a good eye for young comics and because of that good eye, he was known for linking up with or bringing along an up-and-comer for appearances like this and getting them a spot in his contract. Almost everyone in Hollywood has some sort of reputation and it is on that reputation that they get by, not many however have one of generosity like that of Aubrey Clark.

"Don't let anyone ever tell you it's all one in the same, (those shows). The people who say that, *come-off* as if it's the same thing each and every time. So never think that! Never act like that! Every spot, every show, every sixty dang seconds you have in front of another person holding a camera should be a chance at something new. It's all about opportunity. That's the nature of this business isn't it?" continued Aubrey.

"Jesus, did you smoke a joint by yourself before you sent Bruce for me?" asked Eddie semi-rhetorically and referring to the jittery bunch in front of him. Aubrey was quick.

"Absolutely! I smoked one with Bruce when I told him, and then told him to go get you. Bruce is going to do a few minutes with me when I go on. We've still yet to figure that out but hey! Eddie, she really digged you man. I mean it, she told me herself. She was surprised to see me obviously but she said she had a great time watching your set and she'd be in touch."

"Wait, she said she'd 'be in touch?' That's great! You didn't tell me that part! Good job, bro!" shouted Bruce as he passed Eddie the joint with excitement. Eddie however, did not share in their excitement nor did he still have that same gleam in his eye that he did a few minutes ago.

"Come on guys, where do you think we are here?" he said, trying his best to keep in the smoke. As it escaped his expelling lungs he spoke again:

"These are the streets where people come to relinquish themselves to randoms for the chance at eternity. You think I haven't heard the '*be in touch*?' Fuck you bro," said Eddie whilst taking an extra hit for good measure. Aubrey took his turn.

"Do you seriously wanna go toe-to-toe on auditions, *mate*!?" he asked with an ending impression then continued with gluttonous hits.

"I'm dead serious! I go to every audition I can and every time I get snubbed by fucking Leonardo whatshisname or god forbid a Wahlberg wants a part then I'm fucked. I read for: Smoke Signals, October Sky, The Replacements, Ready to Rumble, Bagger Vance, Bring It On, For the Love of the Game, Remember the muther-fucking Titans? This dude fucking-Ryan Gosling too! He's taking everything I read for!" Bruce started to speak but Eddie cut him off and kept listing:

"Small Soldiers, Newton Boys, Wild Wild West, some Scorsese pic in New York and Antz? I didn't qualify to be the voice of a fucking *ANT*? DUDE! Gimme that joint, dammit," shouted Eddie as Bruce pulled away. "Oh, and The Sixth Sense—" but Aubrey cut Eddie off.

"You auditioned with Shyamalan? What'd you read

for the kid or Bruce Willis?" he asked with a pursed smile. Eddie returned with the bird.

"There isn't a damn thing you can say that will make me feel bad for you, man. I can honestly say that I've been out here embarrassing myself a lot longer than you and..." Bruce took a long, solemn pause in between puffs. Eddie sarcastically placed his hand on Bruce's shoulder and said:

"It's okay, big guy. Let it out." Bruce swatted away the pseudo-sympathy.

"Any role I ever read for and even came close to..." Bruce took a big breath, Aubrey and Eddie almost expected a salty tear to fall next.

"Every one, I got beat out by Robert Pastorelli. I'm not kidding dude, every god dang one!" he shouted in a crossfaded stupor.

Suddenly Penny hopped out of nowhere. "Hey motherfuckers!" she yelled. There was still a few hits left on the joint and they let her partake. Whether it was due to that kind gesture just there or if it was predetermined, she removed something from her pocket and presented it to the crowd of four. "Who wants to drop acid?" she asked, with a devilish grin and dangling the small sandwich bag holding micro-scraps of square-cut paper.

EARLY WEDNESDAY MORNING

2:46 A.M.

"Not for me thanks," stated Aubrey with an interception of the joint. He finished it and then squashed it under his shoe. Penny, Eddie and Bruce all raised their hands.

"But I bought four tabs?" mumbled Penny with a puffy lower lip and eyes as big as the moon.

"Ask Lee. Hey Poe!" said Aubrey before being stopped and shushed by Penny.

"No!! Not him come on dude we're trying to chill and have a good time," Penny exclaimed.

"Stop it, he's a good guy and he can *chill* just fine. Hey Poe! Come here a minute and raise your hand!" Aubrey shouted through the now semi-crowded back parking lot. His enthusiasm to include an outsider gave the gang pause. Leland Poe walked over to the gang with that same shit-eating grin. Even though he quite literally had been summoned; Penny, Bruce and Eddie disliked the way Leland always looked as if he's been summoned. As if his presence was necessary for all noteworthy things to occur and all things should cease and then commence on his arrival. He approached with his nose raised. It was disgusting. They caught him up to speed and he was surprisingly down and Aubrey bid them adieu as only chaos would ensue.

"Bruce, once you're back on land, call me," said Aubrey, motioning to his ear with his thumb and pinky extended.

Shortly thereafter the four travelers swallowed their tickets, hopped into Bruce's station wagon and were off towards Malibu before they peaked. The traffic was dreadful but the lights screaming passed them on Sunset seemed to take away from whatever tethers commuter-Earth had planned for the night. Figures began to track across the road and then flicker into the distance or behind buildings. It was an un-recommendable dance only those stoned on the road will know, a hornet's nest of paranoia. They pulled into the empty parking lot of Pepperdine University and sat out on the ocean-facing grass. Those hills quickly melted into a sea of green swords and harmful thoughts for Leland and Bruce, must've been something about the combination of fresh cut grass and sea breeze. Penny and Eddie felt best not to follow them as Bruce chased Leland off into the night. One way or another they found themselves in the sand down by the Malibu pier. Eddie inhaled the freshest gasp of air he had ever taken.

The smell of the dirty mush pushed in from the tides that crept along the underside of the pier and its old wooden beams before vanishing into the wandering mind of Eddie Mason. He watched an otter pick at the barnacles stuck to the base of one pole and a crab grasping for dear life on another. He waved his head over towards the sky and watched the stars twirl for him.

Penny's trip started later than the rest. The sand cold underneath her feet and in between her toes pushing her over the edge of clear-headed. She looked up and saw no stars at all, the night air forcing itself across every nook and cranny of her vulnerable face. Penny turned to her left and relieved herself of her breakfast, lunch, and dinner. By the time she kicked some sand over it and stood back up she was facing the pier and fell victim to the enchanting lights along it. Lamp posts marched along like soldiers in the night before toppling off the end and into the black Pacific. She walked towards the pier like a war-journalist as soldiers above her continued to march towards their dead end.

Bruce finally caught up with Leland running along the Pacific Coast Highway. Lee turned around in terror and shouted:

"Where's our car?! I've never even *been* to Arizona!" Bruce grabbed him by the shoulders, dripping with sweat like a honey-baked ham and tripping his balls off.

"I DON'T KNOW!" he stated urgently. Suddenly, Bruce looked off into the distance and saw a ship out on the coast. His excitement increased until they started to dredge through the ice plants separating the sand and road. Bruce started laughing frantically.

"Aha! It's the Navy! We're saved! Come on Lee we're saved!" shouted Bruce with Leland crying behind him. As they neared the tide Bruce burst into tears along with his friend as the boat had disappeared. He and Leland embraced on the wet shores of their lost island. They cried together and then started cursing the horizon and its fucking boats. Their fit of rage depleted and they walked back up the beach to collapse into the sand. Bruce wiped the sand off on the only clean part of himself and looked over, wiping his tears, to see Eddie lying in the sand no more than twenty yards away. Eddie noticed the commotion and was now looking over.

"Found'em!" he shouted with a limp hand out to point. "Hey, hey! Why?" shouted Eddie with pause. Bruce couldn't speak but somehow Leland managed to, amongst his heavy falling tears.

"Why whaat?" he cried. In return, Eddie only blinked. Then responded,

"Why are you crying?" Leland broke down again into a heavy wail. Bruce calmed himself just to murmur out: "We're stuck here."

Eddie wobbled up onto his feet and then sank down a foot into the sand. "Not anymore you're not," he stated before leading them on a mission to find Penny, their long lost friend. Eddie rallied his troops and helped them clean themselves off before approaching the underside of the pier itself. A farcical venture so formidable it reshaped reality in front of them. What appeared as an arduous and blind mile long journey was actually a 10-15 yard shadowed distance under the bottom of the pier. If they were to cross it they needed to be ready.

"Wait, Eddie," said Bruce with a heavy hand on his shoulder. "You'll need this," he said while presenting a lighter. Eddie took it like a knight before battle.

"Thank you," he returned with his own valiant hand upon Bruce's shoulder. Eddie turned around and took the first steps into sand that the moon's light could not reach. He tried the lighter but it wouldn't strike. A chill slithered down his spine to try again and then once more, still nothing. Ain't that some shit, he thought.

With two behind him, Eddie engulfed himself in the deep dark shadows under the pier. The tide pushing itself closer and closer towards him like a foam-headed territorial defense.

"Hey, before we go any further I need to get something off my chest. I'm really scared and I don't know if I'll get another chance to say this. I really idolize you guys, I act like I don't and I act like I don't care about anyone but it's a gimmick but more of a defense mechanism. I just don't...I don't know, I just wanna be like you guys," Leland admitted.

"And also, it's true what they say. I am getting as much pussy as they say, I'm at like six numbers per show that are at least semi-reliable," continued Leland.

Eddie saw an opening and chimed in,

"One more and you'll have a whole person to call, bud.

Good job!" They cracked up but Leland remained serious.

"See you guys are just jealous, by the next time you boys get any I'll probably be tired of pussy," claimed Leland.

"Yeah and then you'll try penis. It's fine dude not everything's about you," stated Bruce.

"Yes it is! I mean..." Leland caught himself red-handed. Possibly because of the statement or possibly because of a mysterious sound nearby. They pressed forward, Eddie mumbling something to himself with each step. One more step and a giant rat jumped out from behind a post with a piece of trash in it's mouth and scurried off into the shadows. The three knights exhaled and embraced. They got themselves together and continued on their journey to find the holy grail of a person. As moonlight approached them a fear overtook them. These three knights had acclimated to the dark caves of this journey and feared what lay beyond those already deadly shadows. Light became the new unknown, until the jump was made and they approached the nearest lifeguard station as it showed some signs of life in the dead of night.

"Halt! Go no further!" shouted out a harrowing voice. "Who goes there?" it asked again. Eddie stepped forward in the sand to confront it.

"We are but three knights in search of a fair maiden. She means much to us I assure you, and if you are willing to provide any information at all to her whereabouts it would be greatly appreciated!" he shouted before drawing a long silence. Eddie then took a whiff of the scent piercing through the night's breeze.

"Also if you're willing to share in some of that pot it would also be greatly appreciated. We have a long journey ahead of us," he said.

"What does this fair maiden look like?" asked the lifeguardian hut dweller.

"Well it may not need to be said but she is white as fuck! But still quite a sight for a blurry eye if not a sore one," shouted Eddie then tapped Bruce in the chest.

"And she's incredibly funny. She will brighten the darkest days imaginable and she's got a fantastic ass!" admitted Bruce before being cut off by Leland:

"Yeah and she gave me a handy one time outside of Tucson," he claimed. Suddenly, a head popped out from within the lonely lifeguard hut, it was Penny and she was furious.

"What the fuck you lying prick! I'll kick your scrawny little ass! And guess who doesn't get any pot?" she shouted with a childish sad face to force the ultimate amount of shade Leland Poe's way. They huddled in the hut and passed around the smoke, skipping little ol' Poe. Penny grabbed the pipe like a pro and put on an exhibition. "Grass skyrockets your acid trip so don't smoke too much, just enough to bump you back up to seeing swirls," she said before ridiculing Leland's tolerance levels. A harmless prod due to him still recovering from his ego death.

"Ya know, yeah. That's what it is! That's why you get so much pussy, dude. They see you and look at your face and see themselves in you and it just attracts."

The hut broke down in laughter, all except for little boy Poe. They extended the trip for however long it took to find the car again and then drove back to Bruce's via Topanga Canyon. As the Acid wore off the four of them finally found the will to sleep and didn't wake up until sixteen hours later sprawled across various parts of the tiny Burbank apartment.

THURSDAY MORNING

10:50 A.M.

When Eddie finally awoke from his tomb of unconsciousness he sat up to see Bruce was still out cold with his mouth agape and snoring. Leland must have gotten up at some point and left because the only place he could be and not be seen was the bathroom and that door was open. Eddie noticed Penny roll over under her blanket. He leaned over, tapped her on the shoulder and whispered, "Hey, let's go get some grub. I'm starving."

She denied any and all urges to go anywhere but as soon as Eddie mentioned Cupid's hot dogs, she was on her feet with her shoes on and half-way out the door. Eddie tip-toed over to Bruce's disheveled frame sinking into the futon. He reached down and removed a few tattered greenbacks from Bruce's pocket then swiped the keys from off of the kitchen counter. The two rebels drove the stolen station wagon about fifteen miles on the 101 freeway before taking exit 25 to Winnetka Ave. The Northridge location was a bit closer to the apartment but Eddie always preferred the dogs from the corner location in Canoga Park, right by the Canoga Bowl.

They took another right on Vanowen Street and pulled into the mini-lot. A young girl with short blonde hair rolled and danced across the pavement with her rollerblades and high socks. They approached the counter and ordered six chili dogs while Eddie regaled Penny with stories of his childhood in the area. Hot summer days, encased in the San Fernando Valley heat, sucking every drop of sweat out of him and his friends until they heard the ringing atop the door at the local corner store. Bikes laying on their sides or leaned up against the quartz colored stone walls of—pick a store. From sticker covered windows to overdressed street dwellers in jackets and sweats. They would ride along cars nearly clashing spokes with a bass-booming truck scraping its way across the heavily engraved pavement. The valley had it all.

Three of those chili dogs were eaten there on the nostalgically filthy tables while fighting off the pigeons with each bite. They took the other three home, placed two on the counter for Bruce and then Eddie sat down in front of the tv, with Penny beside him, to finish his third dog watching a rerun of Nash Bridges.

"So you figure out how to end that joke yet?" asked Penny with a flick of her lighter to spark up a freshly ground and packed bowl of green.

"No not yet. I just can't figure out how to get there, you know?" he responded. Suddenly, a gregarious roar came over the apartment and Bruce's seemingly lifeless corpse rose from the blanketed ashes of slumber. He let out another deafening yawn and then asked for a hit before stopping in his tracks and following his own nose to the kitchen. Eddie and Penny half expected Bruce to find a cartoon pie in the kitchen, the way he was hunched forward in his aromatic stride.

"These for me?" he grumbled.

"You know it, bud," replied Eddie without looking away from the television. Bruce stood at the kitchen counter and stuffed his face with one chili dog and then the other. Not a second passed and he was already back to the futon asking for another hit. The three compadres began to discuss their plans for the day, all three were off work and had no definitive schedule as acid was all they had thought about for the past 24 hours.

12:42 P.M.

"Jesus, it's almost one o'clock. You wanna stop by the club or we can just fuck around here?" offered Bruce.

"Or we could head back to Malibu and just screw around there, how's that sound?" asked Penny. All hands were in and soon they found themselves back on that same Malibu sand. Bruce had misplaced a lucky coin and was trying his best to retrace his steps along the shore to find it. Eddie found what seemed like the same spot he sat the night prior and took a seat. He sat there in silence before pulling out a lone joint that he had been given by Aubrey after their road trip up North. He fired up and inhaled deeply; although, just as he did a man sat down beside him. It was neither Penny nor Bruce but Eddie didn't seem to care.

"Care for some company? I sure could use somebody to talk to," said the man. Eddie didn't look over, only replied politely and continued to hit the joint. "You know, I come out here sometimes to clear my head too. I always say when life gets to be too much for ya, always find the horizon. It will never let you down and it'll always be there. Stickin' itself out for you without you ever asking for it. After that, everything else seems so small..." said the man poetically. Eddie kept his glazed eyes on the saturating horizon with Bruce's silhouette in front of it pretending to hold a microphone and practicing his act for Kilborn. Eddie offered the joint to said man but he declined.

"I'm on a T-break right now, trying to do what's best for myself and the band. Anyways, thanks for the talk man. I needed it. See ya around Eddie," said the man as he rose from the sand and walked away along the tide. As he did, Eddie looked up to place a face with this unusually polite man's voice and that's when he saw who he was really talking to the whole time.

Back in the car on the drive now towards Santa Monica, Bruce stopped at a light and adjusted his rearview mirror to talk.

"Ey Eddie, who was that you were talking to? On the beach," he asked.

"You'll never guess," replied Eddie. Penny cracked a challenging smile and shot back with,

"Oh yeah?" They played the guessing game for a while before Penny begged him to spill the beans. "Anthony Kiedis," said Eddie. The light had just turned green but Bruce stopped the car in the middle of the intersection to turn around in his seat.

"From the fucking Chili Peppers?!" he shouted. Eddie assured them it was indeed the frontman and then described their chat in loose detail. Bruce turned back around and proceeded through the intersection amongst a chorus of car horns and insults thrown from every open window. They stopped after finding a place to park for free and walked back to the Third Street Promenade. From beatniks to buskers, drummers and dreamers, they had arrived at a non-stop shop for those in search of prime people watching.

They found a reputable bar nearby, a few drinks turned into many and by six PM they were drunk and walking to another spot in Mar Vista and by nine they were completely shit-housed at a Speakeasy in Marina Del Rey. They migrated through the coastal West Side of Los Angeles like beach adjacent birds in a flock of three.

By nightfall Bruce's deserved celebration had become a blackout and he was being helped around by his friends until finally they were thrown out due to Bruce's belligerence. He had become a Weekend at Bernie's impersonator if it wasn't for his ability to speak, however incoherent it came out.

"How dare you! You people don't know who I am! Me! I'm considered royalty all across Madina Rel Dey. I'm a god-damn-comedian!" he mumbled while attempting to remove his clothes. Thankfully Penny caught that one quickly and Eddie called a cab leading to one of the most obnoxious and hazardous drives from Del Ray to Burbank three birds have ever experienced but then again who even remembers these things.

The door slammed shut unintentionally and dropped a picture frame from the wall. It was Bruce as a teenager with his three brothers, a crack in the glass now separating them into two groups of two. Bruce fell onto the futon with enough force to slide it the remainder of the way against the wall then he jumped up and sprinted for the bathroom to projectile vomit across the walls like a regurgitated Jackson-Pollock. Eddie and Penny continued to drink whatever was left in Bruce's stash and smoked the night away. With sand coating their clothes and filling their shoes, the apartment was practically a tiki restaurant minus the good vibes and bad lighting.

FRIDAY AFTERNOON

12:05 P.M.

The following morning, Eddie woke up first once again and retrieved a heaping glass of water from the faucet to quench his thirst. It was even later in the day than it was yesterday so he rinsed his face off with water to start preparing for a possible upcoming shift. That's when he noticed the blinking red light on Bruce's answering machine indicating one if not several missed calls and messages. Eddie attempted to wake Bruce to no avail so he pressed *play* and listened to the first message. The next five messages were just like that first one, all from Aubrey, calling frantically trying to get ahold of Bruce to go over their spots for the late night talk show:

"Bruce I swear to god if you screw me over on this I'll never forgive you. Never! The taping is tonight Bruce.

Call me as soon as you get this. Schmuck!" shouted Aubrey into the phone. He was rightfully furious. Eddie tried once again to wake Bruce but he was in no condition to act like a mature adult, let alone a sober one. The night of hard drinking had been cruel to Bruce and was now taking its toll. With even a slight head tilt he sent himself into a self-propelled vertigo free-fall. Eddie picked up the phone and called Aubrey back using the landline.

"Hello! This better be Bruce!" shouted Aubrey into the phone.

"Sorry no, it's Eddie Mason."

"Kid, just say Eddie. I know who the hell you are. Where's Bruce?" asked Aubrey like a detective on a trail.

"He's not in good shape right now to be honest—" Aubrey cut him off:

"Is he drunk? Hungover?" Eddie looked over at Bruce then responded with a simple

"Yes."

"Jesus, Mary and Joseph, well that's how it goes then. He's out, you're in. I did all I could, they wanted you anyways," stated Aubrey. Eddie was confused.

"What? What do you mean?" he asked. Aubrey then asked if Eddie had even listened to all of his screaming voicemails before calling to which Eddie replied again with a simple,"Yes." Aubrey took a deep breath over the phone and in his politest tone possible explained a scenario where Eddie deletes all of the voicemails left for Bruce and then Eddie gets picked up outside Bruce's place and then takes his spot on the show.

"I'll take care of everything. You've got five minutes right? What am I saying of course you do. Just make sure you're outside for the pick up. Please be there Eddie, I'll owe ya. Not as much as Bruce is gonna owe *me* but still. I'll tell them that he's sick as a dog but you're on the way..." rambled Aubrey, clearly very far away from his phone, before hanging up and making the appropriate calls of his own i.e. his agent, manager and the representatives from the Late Late Show. Eddie kept wondering why Aubrey would owe him for such an opportunity. Was it his reputation? Surely *that* could take a hit. Aubrey Clark wasn't just a household name at this point, he was a rocket in the sky seconds away from his boosters detaching sending him off into space. The cusp of universal fame was at his fingertips from where Eddie sat. Yet here he was, sweet talking Eddie into the spotlight like some guardian angel. He pondered his professional fate and two and a half hours later, Eddie was standing outside the apartment in his nicest pair of jeans, dress shoes and a collared shirt when a black SUV pulled up to the curb. Either that was Aubrey or Eddie was about to get jumped while looking like he was on his way to church.

Thankfully, it was the driver Aubrey had sent and no automatic weapons were inside the vehicle or at least not to his knowledge. He hopped in and they were off to Television City, a lot erected to facilitate the taping and live-filming of various projects for both TV and film. More importantly though, this lot is where CBS presents The Late Late Show with Craig Kilborn.

4:38 P.M.

Upon arrival and check-in Eddie reunited with Aubrey outside his dressing room.

"Okay so here's how it's gonna work. They're gonna call me out to sit down and I'll do my little shtick, answer a few questions, crack a few jokes and then we're going to introduce you after I hype you up to Craig and the audience and then you'll come out, hit your mark and get some laughs for five minutes or so. Nothing too crazy. You've been on tv before right?" asked Aubrey.

Eddie looked down at himself and his current ensemble, implying with his eyes that clearly he had never been in front of a camera.

"Fair point," said Aubrey with a look around the hallway for a wardrobe department. No such luck. Aubrey pulled Eddie into his dressing room and removed one of three blazers Aubrey had brought and set aside for the show. He decided on which one he would don and then gave the next best option to Eddie.

"I look like I'm pretending to go to my dad's work dressed as him," quipped Eddie rhetorically. "Don't say that. You look great. Like a professional! A headliner!" stated Aubrey to ease Eddie's rising nerves however Eddie quickly responded with a middle finger and fuck you, feeling the sarcasm of the headliner quip.

Suddenly, there was a knock at the dressing room door and Aubrey let them in. It was one of the show's producers and the same woman that happened to have scouted them at the store a few nights prior.

"Mr. Clark, wonderful to see you again and thank you again for coming. I just wanted to go over a few things with Eddie. Hi, nice to finally meet you," she said, extending out her hand to shake Eddie's.

"Aubrey initially persuaded me to use Bruce Latto for this spot but unfortunately I heard he's unwell and not going to make it so we're back with our original choice! It's truly a pleasure, we are very excited. Your set the other night was phenomenal and we wanted to check with you and see if you can do that same set tonight for us, if not a little shorter. How's that sound?" she said after adjusting her headset.

"Sure, no problem," replied Eddie as casual as could be to disguise his questioning glance towards Aubrey. Was Aubrey playing them both or was he just trying to boost up Bruce? Eddie thought.

"Wonderful! Now I know why you were the headliner the other night. A real pro!" she shouted with an unknowing twist of the knife with her smile before bidding them both luck and walking away through the crowd of producers' assistants and stage-hands.. No more than two minutes had passed before there was another knock at the door, this time it was Craig Kilborn, namesake and host of the show.

"Two headliners, can't go wrong with that! Thanks for coming guys, I really appreciate it, and it's always good to see ya Aubrey. Happy to finally get you on," he stated with his hand out and a big smile. Eddie couldn't help himself,

"Christ you're tall, what're you like 6'5?" he shouted playfully.

Craig smiled with a wink and said,

"6'7" in heels." Which sent the three of them in stitches. Craig was showing why he was chosen as the host and played along with as much comedic quickness as he had available and that was quite a lot.

"For real though, this is great. I'm excited to have you on, I know Grace just ran you through everything so I just wanna remind everybody to relax and stay loose, okay? Great, let's have some fun. Thanks guys!" said Craig as he left the room.

"See! I told you this was a big deal Eddie," stated Aubrey.

"How could it not be. We're headliners," Eddie replied sarcastically. Aubrey started to assume Eddie didn't know how to take a compliment. Just then Grace knocked on the door again and said. "We're ready for you Mr. Clark."

Aubrey and Eddie immediately looked at each other like a comedic duo.

"Mr. Clark." said Eddie.

"Mr. Mason." said Aubrey and then both walked towards the stage area where shortly thereafter the soundtrack started blaring and it was time for the tiny red lights to shine above those polished lenses.

5:12 P.M.

Out walked Aubrey Clark upon his introduction and the crowd lit up. With each step Aubrey took under the set lights Eddie could feel the rumble of each and every stomping foot in the crowd. His inner richter scale surging, electricity seemed to extend itself out from shoulder to shoulder to erect every section of the crowd and crew until there wasn't a single soul sitting down. Craig and Aubrey shook hands and then they both sat down with their eyes glistening up and out at the rowed faces. Eddie leaned over to the side to watch a small monitor near the break in the curtain. He stared at the screen and what started as a nostalgic viewing of late night TV began to resonate his current reality, illumining the facts and fears of his worst nightmares. What the hell was I thinking? I'm not ready for this! Eddie screamed at himself internally; however, the eyes on the PA next to him almost bulged out of her head before looking over to speak. Eddie sat there within himself, ingesting the throbbing irritation that he may or may not have just screamed his inner thoughts out loud...

"Thank you again for coming by. At this point, I mean honestly I feel like you're *MY* dad. How does it feel to inherent America's youth overnight via basic cable?" joked Craig at the desk. The medium-sized crowd erupted with laughter due to what one can only assume was a giant neon sign to queue for chuckles. Aubrey leaned in his chair towards the desk.

"Of course! This is my first time and I've been dying

to do this, you know I'm a big fan so it's an honor, it's an honor. Plus you're the only guy in the late night game who's so tall his frosted tips are accidental. Truly though, if I'm your father then your mother and I must've met in the Amazon...or maybe a WNBA game, dealer's choice. But I have to admit this new-found fatherhood really comes with some weight, you know pressure and not the good kind of pressure," shouted Aubrey pointing towards his groin. The crowd erupted with even more joy and some became hysterical just because of who said it. Aubrey heard that and dug in.

"Is someone having a stroke back there? I know CPR. Anyways, thank you for having me though, it's great to be here I just got back from a tour through Europe which was really, really cool. We did a-lot-of-shows and I mean a-lot-of-shows and to tell you the truth. I'm tired," spelled out Aubrey to the sympathetic crowd.

"I almost walked into a bar on my way in here... but I ducked.

All jokes aside I did walk into a place near here down the block a touch. Got me a jack an coke... The handjob was fine but the fountain drink tasted kinda funny," said Aubrey hiding a smile. The roof practically blew off the set with laughter, not necessarily because of what was said but more who said it. That was about as raunchy as anyone had heard Aubrey get so it was a delectable treat. Nevertheless Craig reeled them back in with some more questions before going to commercial. Backstage, Eddie was briefed and prepped as he was set to come out just after the commercial break so he stood by the curtain clutching his stomach. His mouth sweating and a torpedo was outbound from his esophagus at any moment. Fire when ready.

They came back from the commercial break with cameras set on the desk reintroducing Craig Kilborn with Aubrey Clark still seated in the chair beside him. No more than two arms' lengths behind them and the curtain, stood Eddie as if anchored in stone, interrogating his inner monologue on why he let himself succumb to the temptations of such an occupation. Gluttonous in its search for glory yet endlessly self deprecating in endurance. All while highlighted under the beaming lights dangling from atop a stage. He felt less like the puppeteer and more like the puppet itself, doing its best to waltz along with broken strings before being singled out as the fraud he truly felt he was.

Just then, he felt his stomach turn again in an overture of harmonic discomfort. It bubbled and swelled beneath his blazer and button-down, convincing him of the imminent purge erupting from within his intestines. Unfortunately and as luck would have it, that's exactly when he was queued to walk out on stage for the very first time.

"Okay, welcome back! Next up we have a very, very funny comedian. You may have recently seen him headlining at The Comedy Store, big shout-out to the Store so let's give it up for Eddie Mason everybody!" shouted Craig and summoning an opening round of applause. Out walked Eddie, doing his absolute best not to look gangly and awkward which as most know is the exact recipe to do so. He stopped right on the yellow T taped on the floor indicating his mark for both the cameras and lights. "Thanks guys," he said into the mic and looking over at Aubrey and Craig at the desk. There was no pre-tape nor rehearsal so Eddie hadn't been out on that stage before that very moment and what he assumed would be a few measly meters between where he stood and the desk, now seemed like miles.

"Now, I know what you're thinking...*is that his dad's jacket?* No it is not... it's my mom's," he said, ushering in air to breathe and hoping that the joke would land before he continued.

"I mean I've heard of a dress rehearsal but I didn't think..." he said while looking down at his gown-like ensemble. A few people in the crowd caught themselves chuckling harder at that than they wanted to and it started to spread. Eddie's nerves started to disappear and he regained feeling in his legs before almost feeling weightless.

"But I'm super stoked to be here. I'm a big fan, and oddly enough a big WNBA fan too so write that down," he said looking over at Craig and Aubrey at the desk, both laughing. And that's when it hit him. Like a warm clairvoyant light cast from above, it wasn't the heat off the stage lights nor the camera operators peering out from the sides of their respective lenses.

His hair was practically re-parting itself an overflow of thoughts swelled from within and fizzled through his scalp. The hairs on his neck and arms began to rise as if called to attention and a cool sensation slithered down his spine. He took a breath in a moment that seemed frozen in time. Cast out alone on the bottomless pit of a stage, with only spoken word or a chord to hang himself yet he felt right at home. A peace enveloped and emerged from his chest and spread across his whole body until he felt shielded by all low-light and pain and simply felt content. Content with being just Eddie, but also a Mason, pressing the nuanced bricks of his craft against each other to form an artistic wall to climb. That's when life pressed play again and he was back to squinting out into the enamored random faces staring back at him.

"Anyways, I've come here in this dress to talk to you about my resumé. Had a couple odd jobs before this, was a waiter for a while. Still not really sure what I was waiting for but obviously it never happened..." said Eddie with a symbolically dry take which led into his bartender joke. The crowd seemed to love it and so did Craig. Unbeknownst to Eddie, Craig gestured to the producer to just let Eddie keep going. They had him on for the set he did at the Store but he hadn't gotten to it yet so Craig rolled the heavy dice on Aubrey's word because the crowd was enthralled.

"Seriously though, I'm glad I didn't walk here in this,

cuz I would've either been cat-called the whole way or kidnapped and I don't even know which one I'd prefer. Probably the cat-calling, but if I'm being honest I'm sure I'll get tired of that too, just like everything else. I'm also tired of defending my out of date news feed. Look at me. I'm a comic. I can't even afford my own blazer so I definitely can't afford to keep buying the paper..

I get all my news from the lady that lives in that van outside the Ralph's on Shoup and Sherman Way. You know the one! Which is fine it's just, if there's ever a major catastrophe... I'm in real trouble.

Speaking of trouble, I don't have a car right now... I didn't at any other point in time before this but I don't have one right now either, which means that I get driven around a lot and because of that I pay for a lot of gas... Why is it so expensive?

I'm about two-blocks and a paycheck away from selling my mouth for a ride man and that is terrifying. Like I'm sure it is for a lot of people. Straight people at least!

But see that's the problem, lemme tell you somethin'. The thing that scares the American population most these days, it's not: terrorism, communism, racism, Somalians, bombs from Iran or Iraq... it's dudes bangin'!

Out of all the world's problems, its trials and tribulations... it seems... this is all man is concerned with as a species. Not space exploration. Not world hunger, health and no child left parentless... just nah, it's the gays. I paid almost 5 dollars yesterday for a pack of cigarettes, the taxes alone lifted my shoes a couple inches which I appreciate but I can't afford a car let alone a whole tank of gas. I'm homeless out here asking for help from that lady in the van and everyone in power is busy bashing the gays. It's gotta stop. Not for them… but for me!!

I want a car. I want an apartment. I deserve to have something to not take care of. Neglect is an American right isn't it? So lower rent and more importantly lower your expectations!" The room sat silent. If the queuing sign was on, then they sure as shit couldn't see it. What would be blocking it? Eddie wondered. Maybe it was blocked by all the smoke from the garbage fire currently flaring on stage, he thought.

"Settle down, settle down. Isn't this a variety show? Maybe we should have the new president on. See if he knows any tricks like the last one. Maybe this one does magic!" he continued to the crowd as they caught up. As Eddie finished the last few bits of his set he felt a strange sense that his tone had change and led him into a different direction. He smiled to pause and place it. Then gathered himself and at the very end when he finally got to the closing joke, his only thought was that the room would fall flat but instead it lit up around him with what he could only assume was just a simple change of vocal inflection. He had influenced his own work to receive a completely different result. For the first time in his arguably-brief career and at the weirdest possible moment for it to happen, Eddie felt like he knew what he was doing. He wondered why the fuck it took a panic attack offstage of his first television appearance to feel that way but hey, if you asked Stephen Hawking he'd say feeling is overrated. Eddie smiled at the crowd and camera and raised his arm to greet those in the back just as attention shot back to Craig Kilborn ushering in another commercial break.

They cut and he waved his hand, calling Eddie over to the desk. They chatted a bit and Craig couldn't have been more pleased with Eddie's performance.

"Get ready kid. You might just be famous tomorrow, I mean this won't air for a day or so but that was great," proclaimed Craig with an honest smile. Aubrey stepped down from the set-stage after congratulating Eddie and proceeded to tell jokes to any crowd member that hadn't ran to the bathroom, in a chance to let out his inner Robin Williams. All of a sudden while Aubrey was a bit further away, Craig pulled Eddie in real close and spoke so softly it was almost a whisper,

"You know I probably shouldn't tell you this but Aubrey gave up the rest of his interview and told me to let you keep going. You know we don't usually do this kinda thing but its Aubrey. You just did about ten minutes on late night tv, and the fact Aubrey Clark is sticking his neck out for you. I just want you to know how big of a deal that is..."

"It's not lost on me, sir," stated Eddie with a grin taking over his face. Craig put his hand on Eddie's shoulder and smiled proudly.

"You're gonna do alright, dude. Just keep being you." Eddie and Aubrey left the set and then passed through the security gate in the same SUV they had arrived in, this time together. Aubrey put a John Prine CD in and lit a fat joint to celebrate. They listened to *Lake Marie* with the windows up all the way home and in that drive Eddie finally captured the essence of who Aubrey really was. A kind, caring human being who also happened to be flawed. It became clear to Eddie that Aubrey hadn't planned nor plotted out his own fame either. One could argue no one can, you just have to stick your feet in the dirt, do what you believe will lift you off into space but no mortal man can plan what to do or expect when you get there. A place where Oxygen itself is overlooked, what's stopping a star from crashing down at any moment's notice. It also became apparent to Eddie, and Aubrey was the perfect case in this example, that most times it takes years of hard work and dedication to become an overnight success and that redundancy is something to really think about.

When they finally got there, the driver was squinting through smoke to see the road in front of him. In short the car had become a proper clam bake. "We're here boss," said the driver. Eddie slowly tilted his head over to look at Aubrey next to him. They both admitted to how high they truly were if it weren't obvious from one seat away and through the smoke. All the while that greatest hits CD continued to play *Picture Show* at a recently lowered volume.

"Hey can I ask you a question?"

"I'm not gonna tell you what was in those bags Eddie," shot back Aubrey in light defense. Eddie laughed and shook his head.

"Nah! I wanna know what Bobby asked you the other night. What's the dirtiest shit you've ever said on stage. Or the worst, you know what I mean," mumbled Eddie in a haze. He sat their with blazing eyes like a vagabond in front of a fire. Aubrey looked over at the clock in the dashboard of the SUV.

9:16 P.M.

"You know what, this was a good day and it's just you and me. So sure...years ago a few buddies of mine had all just got thirty minute specials on Comedy Central, we were hustling you know, living life to the fullest cuz we were full of all that energy and tenacity. I was already a clean comic by then though and relatively known. I got a few little spots in magazines after Montreal and I decided 'Oh what if I release a small special and just go all out.'" He took a long pause in thought and then continued, "Say everything that I've never said before. Just do it in a one night only gig and record it. So we did, we filmed it and it went incredibly well and I was really proud. I was really really proud man, and then I never heard about it again. They canned it; and before you say anything, I've asked multiple people over the years—they claim it's gone so it's over, but anyways! I'll do the bit only because it's all set up...

We had planned a trip—or more accurately a pre-planned bender. We were all going to cop and then meet at my place in West Hollywood, lock the doors and not open them until three days later. Now my one good friend whom I was very close with, both of us were deep in the thralls of our addiction. He had swayed in and out of a pill dependency but at the time we were both quite literally fiending for some white powder and I don't mean Cocaine. He ended up overdosing not long after this but at the time he had just finished a part in a big movie and in the movie he played a homosexual man. The movie was an instant hit. It was funny, he was great in it but when he got to my place he never copped any dope. I love my friend with all my heart... but that son of a bitch! I had already slammed an 8-ball by the time he showed up so I was amped and felt the urge for adventure."

Eddie could see the lights return and surge through his eyes as if memories were being projected against Aubrey's retinas from inside his skull. He watched a true story teller build a world right in front of him. What more could a guy ask for? Eddie thought as he pushed his attention back towards listening.

"Without thinking about it, we left our other buddy there alone in my apartment, hopped in my car and urgently headed to a spot I knew I could score down in Inglewood. It was a narrow drive across long highways that day but we made it. No speeding, no swerving, no cops in sight, thank god. I park up the block from the dealer's pad and now my buddy who's in the car with me starts really freaking out. We're walking towards this dirty apartment block behind a tire shop and my buddy just stops in his tracks. I press him on what's up and call it homophobia, call it immaturity, call it paranoia from the dope but he finally admits to me that he's shit-scared of being thought of as gay, now that that movie is the only place people will know him. The movie where he's a gay man...

I told him immediately that was the stupidest thing I had ever heard in my life and that part of me actually felt bad for him for even thinking that way. It didn't take a psychologist to see how messed up that is on so many levels. He won't budge on his feelings but I forced him to come with me up the stairs anyways so we're climbing up this place and knock on the door. No one answers. I can see the dude inside on an air mattress and I've been there so many times," shouted Aubrey, beginning to feel and re-carve the grooves of his long lost joke.

"I bang on the door again, and again nothing. Finally he peeks his head up to the window and yells something about not wanting to see us. Now I'm getting heated. My high's wearing off and my skins starting to crawl before the crash really hits. I need a fucking bump AND a bindle so I bang on the door and yell: 'C'mon motherfucker this is an emergency!' See, I was already questioning whether or not I fit in with this kinda crowd. I'm not just a stand-up I'm a stand up guy too, I drove a Volkswagen, I come from good cloth. The upward trajectory of my career at the time was in such contrast with where I found myself most days or whenever I had free time. It weighed on me heavily, not just because the risk of dying or contracting some disease. Because it's one thing to do drugs by yourself or with your buddies in the comfort zone of your own abode but when you're strung out and wind up splitting a bindle with a guy you met outside the dealer's house and then black out in an alley. Life doesn't seem so grande..." With each one of Aubrey's words Eddie found himself more and more enamored until his imagination took over and he was now somehow watching Aubrey up on stage, performing the bit with elite precision and unimaginably perfect timing.

"I wasn't quite America's dad yet but I was playing that same type of character on a few shows already. On the up and up, yet I'd found myself down there in Inglewood once again. I really just didn't fit in—at all. So I bang on the door again, 'This is an emergency come on man we've done this dance before don't act like we haven't been here.' That must have set him off cuz suddenly the door rips open except that little chain up top. He shoves his face into the gap like Nicholson overlooking the Stanley Hotel and geez was he loaded. The whites of his eyes were gone completely and I watched them dilate in real time. His facial composition was a science experiment at best.

'The fuck you think you're talking to, huh?' I thought he was going to jump up and beat us with a bar of soap wrapped up with an alpaca scarf and I know what you're thinking... thats blunt forced llama.But he realizes it's me and let's me in but stops my friend. They knew each other too so I was super confused at the dealer's peculiar demeanor. We always had a joke before lighting up; we'd look at each other and go: 'Takes two to tango' and then hit it you know, we had a *thing* so I was super confused.

I took a step back to ask why, and he put his arm out to stop me just like he was doing to my friend in the doorway. He looks at me, then looks at my buddy and then back at me and said: 'It takes two to tango... but I ain't dancin' with no faggot.'

And that is when I knew I was nothing like those people. That's when I knew I wasn't cut out for that life or their company, my presence only furthering the juxtaposition of every shadow I stepped in to. So I stepped out of the shadow, my friend and I left, appalled and offended; and I turned my life around for the better. Plus, if you think for one second that my Nazi grandfather fought in that World War for his grandson or his friend to be called a faggot? I don't think so..." Maybe it was the pot but Eddie sat there speechless. Although entertained he wasn't sure if the joke was over.

"Well don't just sit there, say something!" shouted Aubrey with what almost seemed like a touch of insecurity. Eddie still internalizing each line in order to give a proper answer, he sat there almost confused if it was really as bad as he thought it was. He wondered why the network wouldn't put out any of Aubrey's material, let alone a one-night-event styled special where he let loose. But also Eddie broke down the joke itself and tried to put himself into the wingtips of said producers. What was so bad about it? Plus he's quoting some trashed junky in a bad part of town and during a low point in his life. Are we not allowed to have low points or even more oppressive are we not allowed to talk about them if we do? Then Eddie thought maybe a network promoting the special and having their quickest rising star at the time claiming he is the descendant of a member of the SS wasn't such a great idea. One could surmise that would ruffle some feathers when attempting to lock in the role for a family man with a life and a wife with kids in the suburbs on big network television. Eddie still couldn't really find the right response.

"And they never put it out? What the fuck man," sided Eddie with a sunken brow.

"Hey don't get sad about miss-happenings in *my* career. You keep on and you'll have those same opportunities of your own," said Aubrey prophesying an abundance of overcome-able failures in Eddie's young professional future. Eddie smiled and thanked him again for the opportunity.

"It's been a pleasure. Oh shoot! Eddie before I forget, I'm having a big party tomorrow night. You should come, I want you to be there," shouted Aubrey with some encouraging words before the SUV sped off.

10:22 P.M.

Eddie walked into Bruce's apartment to see Penny sitting on the futon smoking a bowl.

"How was it!?" she shouted with excitement.

"What are you doing here?" he asked.

"Vinnie-boom-botts over there ran outta cat food," she said explaining that Bruce was still too out of it to run his own errands. Thats when Bruce shouted from his bed of blankets,

"I'm not fucked up! I'm hungover!"

Penny turned back to Eddie and said "Whatever. So how was it?" Eddie emptied his pockets onto the kitchen counter and took a hit from the pipe after more egging-on by Penny.

"It went great. I ended up doing like double my time," he replied. She almost cut him off.

"You went over?!" Thinking he mistakenly took more time allotted which is obviously taboo. "No!" Eddie replied before clarifying that they actually let him. Penny almost didn't believe him. They took a shot of whiskey as Eddie explained the full set from start to finish and it finally set in. Penny was proud of him and she hadn't even seen the show yet.

"So when's it air?" she asked.

"I'm not sure. Either tomorrow night or the next maybe?" he replied.

The two peers spent the rest of the night celebrating and Penny made sure Eddie felt recognized after his first television appearance even though he avowed that he wasn't interested in watching it. As complicated as it sounds, in adulthood Eddie was confident but as a professional stand-up he had evolved into the complex of Jonah and his achievemephobia was emanating for all to see after this great feat of success.

SATURDAY MORNING

10:31 A.M.

The next morning, Bruce was up early and making eggs. Eddie complimented the smell emanating from the kitchen. "Well there's only an egg for each of us," stated Bruce transferring the excess yoke from his palm to his pant leg.

"Real generous," added Penny without even opening her eyes. They consumed the egg trio and then cleaned up the mess from the night before.

"C'mon boys. I'll buy ya a real breakfast," Penny stated with a sarcastic glance towards Bruce. The mild, mid-day wind blew through the lowered windows of Penny's '97 Explorer. Leaf green, her pride and joy, it stormed down Balboa Boulevard towards Roscoe and then peeled into the alley on the right. She applied her cherry red wheel-lock and escorted the boys towards the shaded front entrance.

Lulu's Restaurant and Sports Bar across from The Home Depot in Van Nuys was a nonstop shop for good eats and eavesdropping. If the old folks next to you weren't part of the golden age of Hollywood then chances are their kids and / or grandkids are in the business now. Business being show-business because there's no business like it.

"What can I getcha hun?" asked the server. Bruce's eyes were stampeding across the menu like Bison on the Great Plains so she skipped him and asked the same question to Eddie then Penny before circling back a full round robin until all were ready and then drinks arrived. Bruce took a long sip of his hot coffee, sat it down gently on the table and cleared the gunk from the corner of his lips. There was something coming and the whole table knew it. "Alright, I'm askin'. How was it?"

"How was what?" replied Eddie, holding in a face to contain himself. Bruce shoved him towards the end of their booth.

"C'mon man! Don't make me beg, I feel bad enough," he proclaimed with Penny laughing across the booth from him.

"It was great man. It was really really great," said Eddie honestly. Bruce repeated that back almost to himself and then sulked down into his own lap.

"Can I be honest with you about something?" he asked before continuing, it's a weird thing to say out loud but I'm having a really tough time being happy for you, considering the circumstances and all. I know it's my fault and I should've been more professional but fuck man. That could've been my shot." Suddenly the server appeared and began placing plates. Bruce was first and wasted no time digging in, his hunger now highlighted and circled. A steaming plate of pancakes and sides was effortlessly placed in front of Penny and she grinned like it was picture day.

"Mmmmm I love me some *this place...*" she said goofily and as the final plate was supposed to land smack dab in front of Eddie, he looked down to see a knife and fork with a napkin underneath. No plate.

"Sorry hun yours'll be out in a minute mmkay?" the server said as she hurried away to another table. Eddie looked around at the animals consuming their meals, he gulped at the scent of near sustenance. His stomach growled as if trying to usher the beasts next to him into parting ways with a bite, to no avail. He looked up at Bruce to see him wiping egg from his face and picking up from where he left off."I guess I get it.. *He* asked *you*, right? You need a shot too, and it's not like I'm trying to harbor bad feelings. You're pretty much my closest friend so I guess I don't know *what* I feel. Is it shame? Jealousy? Guilt? Was I just hungry? Is it both?" Bruce trailed off back into the rest of his food.

"Geez Bruce, if you're gonna argue do you at least mind giving me a turn?" asked Eddie before his eyes dashed towards Penny's plate next to him.

"I'm sorry," said Bruce.

"No, I'm sorry. I just felt like it wouldn't be that big of a deal," Eddie confessed.

"I guess I didn't think it would be either," admitted Bruce with a heavy tone and embers of deceit still smoldering in his heart. The server returned and placed down Eddie's crackling hot breakfast, he hardly even looked at it. Eddie furrowed his brow and sat there with a poignant pause. He was taking in the information the best he could whilst still enduring the aromas of pork, fried eggs and potatoes surrounding him and taking over his sinuses. Penny watched on amused and eating while Eddie explained that he looked up to Bruce in a way not too dissimilar to the way he saw Aubrey. If not for the glitz, the glamour and flashes for every picture taken; they were both role models to young comics, namely Eddie Mason. "You know that right? I met you and everything changed. I got a best fucking friend out of it sure but I got a fucking mentor too. I know you don't think about yourself the way *we* all do but shit, man—like it or not this is how it played out for me. So give yourself some more credit." Eddie paused once more with a thousand words behind his eyes after filing them down to just a few.

"I didn't know you felt like that. I'm a little caught off guard if I'm being honest," responded Bruce, hoping his skin wouldn't flush if it wasn't rosy already. Penny found herself in a bit of a pickle. She agreed with the sentiment but couldn't quite give her input due to the table's humid turbulence. Against all inner judgement, she decided to jump in:

"Does it make you feel old?" she asked with a heartfelt chuckle to cut the tension. Bruce extended his mug to the passing server holding a coffee pot. She graciously poured his cup to the rim and whispered, "Enjoy." Bruce started to speak in a way that felt forced due to his proximity to the waitress.

"No, it just makes me nervous. How fast life goes around you if you're holding on. I just gotta remember to keep up with it," he said poetically yet yielding not even a glance from said server. Penny made a fart noise with her mouth and threw a double thumbs down in his direction. And with that, Bruce was back to his chipper self. Plates chimed out along with the cutlery as they scraped across each other or onto the table with ecstatic intent. Bruce then owned up to himself in front of Penny and Eddie by regaling them with his discovery that he is going bald and how he found out.

Bruce tapes all of his sets, every single one. Bruce also has a joke where he fights his older brother over an imaginary tv remote and for the bit, he acts it out on stage. Well, while doing so he turned his back to wherever the camera was set up and illuminated for an ever approaching eternity—one big beautiful bald spot.

"That's gonna be a great bit though.." quipped Penny. Bruce exhaled from his nostrils like a bull in heat.

"It better be," he said now knowingly wearing the permanent and ever-growing yarmulke of untanned skin atop his head.

The conversation that followed was only semi-audible due to the stuffing of whatever food was left, down their throats.

"So you gonna go to the party tonight?" asked Penny.

"Eh, I don't know honestly. I work tonight," replied Eddie.

"What party?" inserted Bruce with clear urgency. Bad move, thought Eddie and Penny, so they just ignored him.

"Yeah same here. Like, I really wanna go but not enough to lose a spot. Ya know?" Penny stated with a big gulp of her coffee.

"For real. Who wouldn't wanna go to that? But still," said Eddie, stoking the fire.

"Wait, what party!?" inserted Bruce once more. Again, his question went unanswered and his blood begin to boil.

"I think if I didn't work tonight then absolutely I'd go, ya know?" Eddie said rhetorically.

"I swear if one of you doesn't tell me what the fuck's going on!" shouted Bruce at the top of his lungs, singling out their table in the restaurant. Eddie calmed and quieted him down like a runaway hound before finally spilling the beans to quell the barking dog.

"Aubrey's throwing a party tonight for the release of his thirty-minute special and then the talk show appearance we did, that airs tonight too so..." Eddie trailed off.

"Oh I'm so fucking going," stated Bruce matter-of-factly whilst stealing a piece of toast off Penny's plate.

"Dude you work tonight," said Penny before Bruce made a childish face.

"Does it look like I care? I'm not trying to miss a party at fucking Aubrey Clark's house! Are you kidding me?" he shouted in an attempt to gain attention and clearly ignoring his feelings for the lack of an invitation. Penny then called Bruce a palindrome of a person, leaving him lost for words and clueless.

"It means you're the same thing standing up as you are upside down—pubis," she stated with a smile only she could create.

Bruce then called over the server and ordered three shots of whatever liquor they had available and as they were still questioning him for it, the shots arrived. Obviously Lulu is quicker with the liquor than she is with a pork breakfast but who's counting. Penny and Eddie declined their shots although Bruce had other plans.

"They're not for you," he said before shouting "Hair of the dog baby!!"

"It's noon, man," stated Penny as she signed the merchant copy of the check. They stood up from the booth and from there to the car they were pestered by Bruce on every minute detail of the party. All they told him was that "*everyone*" was going. Bruce was gushing with excitement, rose wouldn't show on his cheeks but he smiled from ear to ear until confronting his not receiving an invitation. Eddie looked over into the side mirror and caught a glance of Bruce arguing with himself. The window was rolled down and he wasn't loud enough to eavesdrop but clearly he was in the thick of it with himself. Self-deprivation under the blinding light of the sun through his open window.

They drove back down the street and after a few blocks Bruce couldn't take it. He rolled up his window, seemingly forcing his inner thoughts out and into the wind without any intention of retrieving those thoughts. He was going to that party, no ifs, ands or butts.

His smile returned again as the Explorer pulled into a guest parking spot for Bruce's apartment. They walked inside to see a message on his answering machine. He stepped over and tossed his keys onto the kitchen counter with a slide. He pressed play:

"You disgusting son of a bi-" he skipped the message.

"Still me bitch! What are you gonna do abou-" he skipped the message berating him again, disclosing the troubled relationship with one of his brothers and just after both Penny and Eddie lost interest Bruce, the final message played and a voice they recognized rang out through the tiny apartment.

"Hello... Bruce," Aubrey said like Seinfeld would Newman. "Or should I call you Mister Latto now? You're such a big shot that you no-show me on my own invitation you slimy putz! Well the joke is on you because your replacement was quite a charmer and he may have just gotten himself quite the spotlight too. But he's also your buddy so I want you to be happy for him..."

"I am happy for him!" outed Bruce to his voicemail machine, as if it was going to respond back. Nevertheless, it continued.

"--You'll get'em next time bud. I'll make sure to plug you next time I do anything but we'll figure it out and I'll make it up to you. I promise. Anyways. Uhm, I'm having a party at my new place! I want you to be there. We're gonna put on my thirty-minute special and then we're gonna watch me and Eddie tag-team television.

I invited just about everybody at the Store. You know fucking Karl turned me down? What a douche, right? Okay so be there or be circle and roll your butt home. I'llcallagainlatercuzthemessageislon—" the message ended before he could finish.

Bruce's smile grew so large it was forcing Penny and Eddie up against the walls. He grabbed all of the clothes off of the floor and started to clean up as if the party was in his shitty studio apartment. He practically levitated all the way down the block to do laundry for four hours. Before hovering back with a vibrating glee. Dopamine, what a rush. His cleaning turned to folding once the linens were cleaned and he was then holding outfits up in the mirror and asking Eddie and Penny for advice on different ensembles. This continued in what almost became a montage before Bruce decided on a combination everyone approved of and started pacing, trying to figure out what he was forgetting.

"Oh!" he shouted. "I forgot to get gas!" Eddie and Penny rolled their eyes and continued staring at the television, it's thick back casting a shadow along the wall due to the setting sun forcing itself through the blinds. Bruce grabbed his keys and stormed to the nearest gas station to put $20 in the tank and to empty their shelves of scented hangers for his rearview in what amounted to around five trees and six sets of cherries dangling like dyslexic mistletoe, encased by the windshield from under the afternoon rays.

8:59 P.M.

As the bell toll on nine o'clock, an early midnight breeze blew across the necks of those outside The Comedy Store. West Hollywood was alive and at its best for another night out. Eddie was acting master of ceremonies. The first few hours he was at the door as usual before being pulled by Mitzi. She told him the girl who was supposed to come in didn't show up so Eddie, in an act that was becoming ritual, happily filled the spot. He ran through the room dodging groups of people on his way to the bar for a quick pick-me-up to fuel him through the oncoming performance. His petrol of choice for the night was a cocktail called the Paper Plane which he indeed intended on flying for the rest of the night... Right around then Bruce's station wagon rolled down the street and parked a few houses down from Aubrey Clark's house in Hidden Hills. He was carpooling for Leland and a few other friends that needed rides. They approached the correct number painted on the curb outside the house and started walking up the driveway when the door opened and Aubrey walked out to greet them like a King presenting his castle. He asked them what they thought and a million other questions before showing off the cars in his driveway. They glistened under the night sky and then all calm was penetrated as

Aubrey got in the sports car and revved the engine. He walked them inside and introduced them to his wife and then a few other people in the entranceway before getting them drinks. The place was packed. Athletes, actors, musicians and one or two models. The party was a who's who of everybody from People Magazine to the LA Times. Aubrey grabbed a cold seltzer and gave them a tour of the backyard. "It's glorious!" shouted Bruce like a chubby child in a playground. Aubrey smiled and offered anything they needed before going off to get one of his famous joints.

"Bro!" shouted Leland.

"You made it!" shouted one of Leland's model friends. They walked off to talk to more interesting people apparently in another room.

"Hey! Bruce Latto!" shouted a voice from behind. He turned around to see another guy who typically auditions for the same parts as him and an awkward conversation ensued. On the other side of the room, Aubrey was setting up his tv to make sure it was on the proper channel and then walked back into the kitchen to talk to his wife. They kissed and then he got her a drink from the fridge then went straight back to people pleasing.

10:51 P.M.

Back in the Store, Eddie was walking towards the stage to introduce the next comic.

"It's the headliner!!" shouted Gilda then conducted a round of applause for the boy. He laughed it off and introduced Penny Peterson with all the gusto he possessed.

"Now that's a headliner!" shouted Gilda just to hurt Eddie's feelings. After Penny's set they took a ten minute break and just then, the phone rang.

"Eddie! It's for you!" shouted Kurt the security guard.

"Who is it?" asked Eddie from across the room.

"It's somebody named Vanessa," Kurt shouted back. Without a second to react Eddie leapt across the room towards the phone.

"Hello?" he said, trying his best not to breathe into the phone.

"Did I get ya?" asked Aubrey with a heavy laugh, "What's up man? We miss ya here. I think you're on right now, I can hear them laughing. But I know you're too cool and won't watch it. Anyways you got a minute?" he asked. Eddie exhaled deeply and said, "Yeah, what's up?"

There was almost a pause on the other end of the line before Aubrey spoke up but it was hard to tell over the noise of the Store.

"I'm thinkin' about using. Or just having a drink... We're having a good time and it's all good but... What do you think?" he asked. Eddie was nowhere near equipped for the support needed in that loaded question of a moment but he did the best he could.

"First off, I have to tell you, I'm high as shit right now so you're gonna get high as shit advice," he replied with a smile, wiping the sweat from his forehead with a bar napkin. Eddie smiled at a few passing people and got out of their way and then diverted his attention back to the phone to ask,

"How long have you been sober dude?" diverting the attention back to Aubrey's accomplishments. On the other end of the line Aubrey took a long agonizing breath.

"I'm uhm, I had a mishap years ago but it wasn't a problem. I never told anyone besides my wife, it's been over five. Years."

"So what's making you wanna drink now?" asked Eddie. Aubrey responded quick this time.

"I don't know, everyone's just having such a great time and I, I just wanna feel that again. Not *wasted* just, you know. Sip. Enjoy. What do you think? Should I do it?" asked Aubrey, stammering.

"Dude I'm not really a yes or no guy, you know. My brain doesn't work like that. I think, if this is something, tonight——that later on you're gonna just pretend didn't happen then is it even worth it? Risk rolling that snowball towards the edge of the hill seeing how close you can roll it without it falling down the hill and creating trouble. Is that trouble worth it even with everything you have and how far you've climbed up on that cold hill? The bigger the hill the bigger the trouble man and... Or this will be something you do tell people about later on. About how a call woke you up and marked a moment where you had to make a choice. You know I'ma say not to do it cuz we both know you're going to be cool but after two or three, it's now a problem. Whoever you're with I bet they're stoked just to be with you. How you are now. Not all faded and trying to be funny and shit..." admitted Eddie.

"Okay—what about a cigarette?" asked Aubrey in his typical funny tone.

"Eh, one's not gonna kill ya, Go grab your lady and tell her you wanna share a cigarette with her. It'll be romantic," replied Eddie with the same casual tone he always managed to keep. He could feel Aubrey smile through the phone somehow then Aubrey said:

"Hey I gotta go but kid...thanks. I mean it."

"No problem man. Oh and tell Bruce, Mitzi is pissed he no-showed." Now Eddie heard Aubrey gasp through the phone.

"Is she really?" he asked in shock.

"Fuck no. I doubt she even noticed but *he* doesn't have to know that," stated Eddie with a laugh. "Stay real Eddie. I'll see ya around," said Aubrey with a pause then hung up. He walked back into the living room to find out he missed Eddie's part of the show so he went into the kitchen to finish his conversation from earlier. They were talking about the song *Weatherman* by Hank Williams Jr. and how it somehow is able to manifest the deepest of emotions like a cloud does acid-rain. They mutually agreed to all go out and smoke a cigarette together while listening to the song but Aubrey didn't want to do it without his wife. His happy guests obliged in the loving sentiment and everyone went out into the backyard to wait.

Aubrey took a left down his hallway towards the bedroom. He stepped closer and closer before slowly opening the door to see his wife, ferociously riding Leland Poe in their matrimonial bed. Between the whir of the ceiling fan, the percussion of the box spring mattress and both of their sweat soaked moaning, Aubrey was just a fly that crept in on the wall to them having the erotic time of their lives.

The bedroom door slowly closed behind him and suddenly two loud pops rang out from the bedroom, startling those that heard it and freezing those that didn't. Not long after that a third pop sounded off and by then the party's volume had declined enough to send a screaming fit of havoc throughout the Hidden Hills home.

11:11 P.M.

Eddie started to walk away from the phone when Mitzi called him over. She lightly punched his arm and said, "You know somethin' Eddie? All these kids say they wanna make it and they wanna work but then have the balls to not show up for work and then expect to get more and better work. Like that little fucker Poe, I saw him crawling around here somewhere earlier but he's nowhere to be found. Well it doesn't work like that. I appreciate you showing up. You're a good one, Penny was right about you," said Mitzi as she started to walk back to her office.

"Wait what did Penny say about me?" he inquired anxiously.

Mitzi turned around only halfway and without dropping a beat, "She said you're an asshole." Then kept on towards her office. Eddie's watch-timer sounded and he headed back towards the stage with a smile from ear to ear.

AFTERWORD

Comedy isn't a genre. It's not an interest or a career. It's a voice within a space. A space that if you aren't there to experience it at the right time in life then you might miss it. Some things age out and realize the ignorance in those ways and other things seem to age with dignity because they cannot ever be understood as untrue. Truth can be just as funny as fiction however it is fiction's purpose to challenge that with which you question its reality. That is what a joke is. A pickle between propaganda and a white lie, the combination of truth and speculation to guide you on a conspiracy called psychology, mathematics through chemistry, and anthropology all to understand something from a different point of view with less paperwork. You don't have to like the point of view but you're going to understand when you are told how cold it gets when you can't afford a heater in the winter or how hot it gets when you can't fix your AC in the summer. Because as humans we can't live life without that curiosity, of knowing what it's like. Whatever *it* is.